THE EDGE OF LIMITS

IF NOT ME, WHO?
IF NOT NOW, WHEN?

S J GERVAY

The Edge of Limits published in 2022
by Flying Elephant Media
P.O.Box 1069 Bondi Jct
NSW 1355 Australia
flyingelephant.com.au

Cover design by Lauren Esdaile

The moral rights of the author have been asserted.

First published Australia in 2002
by HarperCollinsPublishers Australia Pty Ltd
ABN 36 009 913 517
www.harpercollins.com.au
Internals designed by Lore Foye, HarperCollins Design Studio

Cataloguing-in-publication data:

Gervay, Susanne.
The Edge of Limits
For young adults
ISBN: 978-0-6482035-5-1
1. Consent – Fiction. 2. Teenage boys – Fiction. 3. Teenage girls – Fiction. 4. School camps – Fiction. 5. Interpersonal relations in adolescence – Fiction.

ISBN: 978-0-6482035-5-1

Printed and bound in Australia

sgervay.com

‘When they go low, we go high.’
Michelle Obama, first African-American woman to serve as the first lady of the USA

To my nephews Leonard and Paul Gervay,
my son James Ruben and daughter Tory Gervay.

Your grandfather Zoltan Gervay
would be so proud of you today.

Praise for *The Edge of Limits*

'. . . an authentic trip into an adolescent male mind. . . refreshingly honest and beautifully written.'
Sydney Morning Herald

'Confronting in many ways, this novel. . . will certainly find an audience to which it can speak.'
Viewpoint

'. . .An epic story, beautifully written with clear spare prose and the ability to go right to the heart of young males in modern society.'
Carol Kayrooz, University of Canberra

Acknowledgements

The Edge of Limits is a brave journey into consent. One that I could not have done, without my son's insights and honesty. I 'sucked' out his young adult brain and his stories of mateship, partying, parental expectations, betrayals, love and relationships with girls. I learnt to rock climb, badly. Put up a tent, not too badly. Climb to the top of a mountain and contemplate who we are. He sent me on a pathway that unlocked the great issues of courage, power, peer group pressure and love. We all want love, but how to get there? I am glad my son has found his true love now, but what a rugged ride.

I also could not have gone on this journey without my daughter, who shared her stories and observations with insights and honesty. The stories of girlfriends, family, dating, love, coercive control, assault, rejection and that devastating impact on self-esteem. Then there is consent. What is it?

I thank the generosity of my son and daughter for giving me the authenticity and understandings to write *The Edge of Limits*.

Susanne Gervay

Other books by S. Gervay

Shadows of Olive Trees

That's Why I Wrote This Song

Butterflies

Heroes of the Secret Underground

I Am Jack series:

I Am Jack

Super Jack

Always Jack

Being Jack

Picture Books

Ships in the Field
illustrated by Anna Pignataro

Gracie and Josh
illustrated by Serena Geddes

The Boy in the Big Blue Glasses
illustrated by Marjorie Crosby-Fairall

Elephants Have Wings
illustrated by Anna Pignataro

Indian-Australian Anthologies
edited by Dr Sharon Rundle and
Professor Meenakshi Bharat

Fear Factor: Terror Incognito

Alien Shores

Relatively True

CHAPTER 1

Bags, guys, parents, teachers are already outside the front gates. There's that moron, Watts. He looks like a commando. He must have raided the army disposal shop. I bet those leather boots have metal tips on them. Great for kicking guys when they're down. His brainless mates are with him. He'd be piss-weak without them hanging around. Mum's driving me to the bus. What is she saying?

'Have you got everything, Sam? Did you remember your insect repellent? Sunscreen?'

'It's fine. I can pack you know.' I rub my chin. I've started shaving. Well, once a week anyway. Grandpa left me his shaving brush. He made the handle out of cedar. The cedar is smooth, with his initials engraved into it. The bristles are soft, not like the cheap commercial ones with plastic handles. Every Sunday, after my shower, I take out my razor blade, Grandpa's brush and shaving cream. I take my time, lather up, spread foam over my face.

Mum parks near the bus stop. I know she wants to wait with me but she can't any more. At least, not here.

'See you later. You'd better go, Mum. You don't want to be late for work.'

Mum has been the bookkeeper in Mr and Mrs Christos's newsagency for as long as I can remember. It has meant we have been the most informed people around, except we're always a day late. You can always find yesterday's newspaper and last week's magazine on the coffee table.

This year I started working on Friday and Saturday nights at Pizza Palace. Mum didn't want me to because she said study is more important. I argued until Mum gave in. I promised I'd study seriously on the other nights. So I'm not broke any more and I met Laura there. Laura. I'm going to miss her.

I tell Mum again that she can't wait. She knows. 'All right, Sam. I'll pick you up at five o'clock next Thursday.' I watch her drive away. She looks back once, waves, then she is gone.

Gone. Eight days. Last year's camp was only three days. I learnt to hate a few guys on that camp and I stank when I got home. No showers and the long drop. I'll probably get through the physical garbage, but living with guys like Watts, that is real garbage. Imagine Mum waiting here to wave goodbye? Sure, if I want to die on the camp. No waiting, because we're men. I look over at Watts. Some are bloody stupid men.

There's Fat George. He'll never make it. The Principal lectured everyone, parents, teachers and students, in the Assembly Hall. Parents were sucked right in when the Principal said that camp 'will improve fitness, as well as socialisation skills. The boys are going to be challenged.' Right, like I can't wait to scale cliffs, burrow through mud holes, grovel into caves, dive into freezing underground rivers. And I can do all this with maniacs, and victims, and guys I don't like or trust. The teachers separate friends. It's supposed to bond you to mankind. I don't want to bond to the mankind I've seen around here. In Watts's case, it's like bonding to a serial murderer.

'Knox, over this way.' That's me. Sam Knox. I'm not Sam here. My mum, friends and Laura call me Sam, but at school I'm Knox. It's a male school fixation to be hailed by your last name. Maybe it makes you an Emperor. Caesar Sam or is that Caesar Salad? I'm tough and I'm Knox. I wanted to go to a co-ed school where I'd be called Sam and where there are girls. The only school around home is single sex, so that's it. Poor Fat George isn't called by his last name. He's called Fat George.

'You're in B group, Knox. Put your bags in that pile and get onto that coach.' Mr Seaten, alias Ape King, ticks off my name. Seaten is built like an orang-utan and has as much sensitivity as one. Maybe I'm insulting orang-utans. He hasn't liked me much since the parent-teacher night. Since that night, Mr Seaten slashes red train-track lines through my geography mistakes, with comments like, 'You don't understand the work, Knox.' He really means that I'm stupid, a loser and a failure. I really like Seaten. Sure.

At the last parent-teacher interview, I begged Mum not to say anything to Seaten. It was the first parent-teacher interview that Grandpa wasn't at. Grandpa always said, 'As long as you do your best, Sam.'

Mum was quiet in the car. I had a sick burning feeling in my stomach. Mum was quiet as we walked into the school hall. I didn't feel like talking either. The hall was crazy with people and the intercom was blaring. I looked at the brown walls and wooden floors. Reminded me of mud. Parents and kids slid like slow slithering blobs towards teachers for the verdict. 'Your son is a genius.' 'Your son is a moron.' 'Your son is . . .' I didn't really care, but Mum did. Grandpa used to take us out for a hamburger afterwards.

A few guys grunted hello. Some parents nodded at Mum. She pretended to smile. Seaten was waiting for us at the Geography table. We scraped the plastic chairs across the wooden floor and sat. I nudged Mum not to say anything, but she didn't listen. Her hands were pressed together so hard that her knuckles were white.

Seaten fingered the names and marks on the class ledger and shook his head. Mum's voice had a crackly edge. 'Sam likes Geography.' Seaten shook his head. 'Sam is good at Geography, like me.' She caught her breath. 'Like his grandfather.' Her hands were nearly transparent as she spoke. 'The past few months have been . . . difficult. Grandpa . . .'

Seaten didn't hear. He just flicked over pages, droned on about curriculum and percentages and failure.

I think about those last weeks Grandpa was in hospital. I don't want to. I try to block it out, but the memories creep into my mind when I'm not looking.

Every day Mum and I visited. Every day we walked through those antiseptic corridors with that cutting smell of bleach. There was always this feeling inside me as we reached his ward. Like a stone in my throat. Grandpa seemed small lying there, alone in a ward of strangers. His black-rimmed glasses were always on the dresser, but Grandpa couldn't see well without his glasses. There was a drip snaking into the back of Grandpa's hand. I hated that. His hands had always been big and capable. Fix-anything hands. Protect-us hands.

They were motionless, blotched purple. But when we came up close, he'd raise his fingers. Just a little.

Seaten stopped talking. He leaned back in his chair with his wiry freckled hands behind his head. 'No. He won't make it at a higher level of Geography,' he said, totally uninterested, and rubbed his after-five shadow. He always looked like he hadn't shaved.

Mum pressed her hands together even harder. She talked, waited, talked, stared, until Seaten started flicking agitated looks between Mum and his watch. He had a football game he wanted to go to, but Mum wouldn't stop talking. It was her bookkeeper's voice, repetitive, as if she was reading out numbers. In the end, he shrugged his shoulders. 'He can do advanced Geography but he won't make the grade.'

Mum cried in the car afterwards.

Bus stop. I quickly look at Seaten's B list. My friends, Andrew and Con are on the A list. Spano's name is right on the top of the B list. I groan. Watts's name is there. The rest of the B list is mainly acquaintances. Guys you'd say hello to when you race past, or kick in the shins for a joke. You wouldn't ask them to your house, but you would go out with them on a Saturday night. Not that I go out much on Saturday nights any more due to Laura and working at the Pizza Palace getting rich. Then there are the Saturday night Rave parties. That last Rave was bad.

'Stop shoving,' I yell at the guys behind me. I get a window seat and dump my bag on the seat next to me — I want to bond with my bag while I can. Andrew and Con climb onto the other coach. A and B groups only meet up after the cave.

The cave. I don't know why we have to go there. Seaten's bloody stupid idea of 'a challenge'.

Andrew sticks his thumb up at me through the window. I do the same back. Con bends across him and sticks out his thumb, too. Andrew punches him, laughing. Andrew was my first friend at school. He only has a mum, like me. He has an older brother as well. Con is different. He is Greek with two parents and two brothers. His parents are really involved in everything he does. I bet his mother packed an extra jumper and made ten sandwiches for the trip. He hates that. I have two ordinary corned beef and mustard sandwiches packed courtesy of Mum. Andrew yells out, 'Don't break a leg,' at the same time as their coach blurts out a fist of smoke. I watch the coach heading away.

My stomach takes a dive. Right. I'm on my own. I stare out of the window trying not to think about camp. I start looking out for old cars. I want to buy a bomb of a car and fix it up when I get off my Learner's driving license in a couple of months. I'll be seventeen and will have wheels.

'Knox, wake up. Move your stuff.' Seaten shoves Fat George at me.

Fat George. I throw my bag onto the floor. He sits down next to me. This is not a good start. I nod, then grunt 'Hi,' and that's it for conversation for the next five hours. The heating makes it warm in the coach and the seats are comfortable. The traffic thins as we get onto the freeway out of the city. The coach driver beeps at a lady driver who is in the fast lane moving at forty kilometres per hour.

'Women drivers are pathetic,' Luke calls out. Then the jokes start.

'Women drivers travel faster in all gears, especially reverse.'

'What's the same about a woman driver and biscuits? They're both crackers.'

'Why are women drivers dangerous? They have in-built booby traps.'

I look at Fat George smiling. He must have a dick after all. The guys at the back are falling over themselves laughing, calling out, 'boobs, breasts, tits, fun bags.' I swear Watts is salivating like a mad dog. They go on about whose tits they have seen, mauled, touched up. Then the morons talk about tonguing it down a girl's throat, getting it up them, doing girls. At the front of the bus, Seaten is thumping his hand against his chest in time with some sort of music coming out of the headphones. The backs of his hands are covered in fuzz. He really is an ape. I turn around and see Watts and the others dribbling over a battered tit-shaped pear.

Tits. I think about tits a lot, especially Laura's. I have a trophy tacked onto my wall next to the 'Oh! Shit!' poster: B cup, black, lacy and satin. Andrew has drooled over it quite a few times. There are a lot of great tits on television — especially the foreign films with subtitles. People think you are smart if you read subtitles. It is such a joke. It is about tits.

When Mum is asleep, I switch on the late night films. They're sexy, especially the European ones. Women strip and so do men and they play around. Usually there is an argument, then making up, kissing, mauling, full frontals, sex and, yes, close-up shots of tits.

Andrew is sex mad and he hacks into the porn sites on the school's Internet. I saw the most amazing things the last time he hacked into it in the library. The sites are very anatomical. Plenty of body parts and coloured condoms.

Something stinks. I look at Fat George. He grunts garlic salami breath at me. 'Lunch,' he splutters.

'Keep your face away from me,' I snarl as I shuffle through my pack for my sandwiches and drink. Everyone is eating except for Bennie who's vomiting into a paper bag.

The orange juice tastes good. I wipe my mouth with the back of my hand, then stare out of the window. The city has disappeared into fields of grassland. There has been rain. I like the green of the flats and the brown of the craggy outcrops behind them. The wheels of the bus whir in quick rhythm as we drive past farms, new housing developments, cattle grazing. The landscape races by like streakers. I grin. Streakers. Everyone was falling over themselves laughing when Andrew threw Con's clothes out of the gym window last year. Con really streaked.

'The Great Dividing Range,' Seaten screams out. I look up. Mountains rise like gigantic walls in the distance. That's where we're heading.

The toilet cubicle at the back of the bus is starting to smell. Missed pees. Suddenly the coach swerves off the freeway. There's a long howl from inside the toilet. Everyone turns around to see Luke struggle out.

'Pissed your pants?' 'Need to look where you aim.' 'Want some help next time?'

'Shut up, you losers.' Luke tosses an empty drink can lying on the floor at a couple of guys. Hits one in the head.

I look at my watch. It's been hours already. How much longer? The bus winds past a sandstone village. The steeple looks like a hangout for the local finches. We're climbing higher and the bus is moving slower as it chugs along. My eyelids close, open. I watch eucalyptus gums shadow the window, then I close my eyes again.

My eyes open with a start. There's a gale in my ear. 'What? What?' I mutter, then I see him. It's Fat George breathing like a pig. I elbow him hard. He shuffles closer to the aisle and it's quiet again.

The coach veers off onto a narrow, winding back road bordered by government-planted pine forests. There are huge tracts of them. I like the smell. Pines. Reminds me of Christmas.

Last Christmas was the first one without Grandpa. Mum cooked the turkey like she always does. Grandpa and I used to put up the pine tree in the lounge room. I did it alone this time. It was harder, much harder. The house smelt of mountains. Grandpa used to tell us one of his famous fishing or camping stories. There were no stories this Christmas. We didn't laugh much and the turkey didn't taste as good. Mum put on taped carols.

The pine forests start to change as the road becomes steeper and more winding. It is wilder, more rugged territory. The bus is spluttering now. Someone calls out, 'We're farting up the mountain,' and there is laughing and a few farts explode from the back. Seaten takes out his earplugs and yells at everyone, 'We're here.'

There is a flat dirt landing ahead. The bus grinds towards it. A woman is standing with her feet apart waving the bus forward. She's wearing baggy khaki shorts over long white thermals that reach down to her ankles. Her feet seem huge with massive army boots that have metal tips which are bigger than the metal tips on Watts's boots. Ropes are hung over her shoulder; a Swiss army knife, a hunting blade in a leather sheath and a torch hang from her black belt. Her thermals cover her arms, and go up to her neck. She definitely has tits.

There are wolf whistles and Seaten tells the whistlers to shut up. The bus stops. The doors open and the woman jumps onto the bus. She looks about twenty-five. She's only about one hundred and fifty centimetres tall, but she seems to take up all the space at the front. 'Get your gear out. Take your bags from under the bus. There are the crates. Carry them. Follow me to the clearing.' I want to laugh. It's a lot of noise from a small, titty instructor. 'By the way, I'm Sarah, your guide for the duration of the camp.'

As Fat George struggles out of his seat, Watts yells at him to move his fat butt. George doesn't yell back at him. He just goes red and blubbery. Seaten is already ordering guys to carry the crates of gear. Someone shoves me in the back. I turn around, snarling. 'Watch it, you bloody idiot.'

He has second thoughts.

CHAPTER 2

Rolls of toilet paper rage through the air like a dance party. Names echo back with each catch. 'Seaten.' Throw. 'Watts.' Throw. 'Spano.' Throw. 'Sarah.' Throw. 'Luke.' Throw. 'Bennie.' Throw. Sarah's tits jut out under her thermals as she tosses three rolls at one time. Names crisscross each other until everyone has called out their name and everyone has a roll of toilet paper.

We need our toilet roll for the long drop. At Base Camp there is a dirt track crawling around the edges of the mountain. It winds down to the long drop. I know all about long drops. You've got to be careful walking that dirt track. Mounds of dried shit and fresh shit hide under ferns and undergrowth. Some people can't stomach the long drop stink and that moment of quiet before you hear the splash or squelch. So they squat behind a tree or bush and, if caught, risk hours of work details as punishment. As your bum nervously sits on the wooden seat, the thought of spiders, maggots, piles of shit and piss at the bottom of the pit wrenches your gut. Some guys don't go at all. For eight days they'll hold it in until their bowels are solid iron. I did that on my last camp. It was only three days of solid iron. I could hardly walk by the third day and slowed the trekking down. The Principal was right. A real socialisation process happened; humanity at its best. I got kicked, shoved, a few stones were thrown, catcalls — 'We'll be late for dinner. Move it, arsehole.' That is funny when you think about it, except I didn't laugh then.

At the end of that last camp it was fairly rotten or fairly ridiculous, depending on how you look at it. The Assassin (or the Instructor, if you want to call him that) asked who hadn't gone to the toilet. As if you'd answer that. Two pathetic, always-tell-the-truth guys said that they hadn't. They were made to have laxatives. Up-their-bum laxatives.

The expedition is 'in the field', so we dig our own toilet at the end of each day except for the first night. That is long drop territory.

Seaten loves all of this. He has been hanging out for the cave — 'It'll prove what you're made of.' Seaten is fit, forty and a fanatic. He always jogs: to school, from school, around the block, up to the top floor of the Science Labs, down at the oval, to the gym. He coaches the senior basketball team and he works those guys long and hard. Long and hard. Hey, a joke. What do a basketballer and a dick have in common? They both work long and hard. Good joke? Or maybe all those late-night movies are turning my brain into mush. God, I hope not. I don't want to be like Andrew. His sex obsession is ruining his life.

Seaten is climbing up the mountain behind Base Camp. There he goes, along the mountain, over the mountain, down the mountain. He is definitely an anthropoid. He's bouncing around the campsite carrying rocks and spades with three lucky sweating guys in tow. At least they're not cold. I am frozen. I have to admit that Seaten makes a good fire: deep hole, circle of rocks, tepee of twigs, dry starter leaves, twigs, branches, and then the big stuff. Logs.

It's getting dark. The fire is spitting sparks by the time Seaten yells out that Sarah is ready to brief us. The heat defrosts my fingers and ear lobes. Grandpa always told me that you have to hold your ear lobes between your finger and thumb and rub them. Otherwise, they break off. He'd rub his ear lobes then. I start to rub my lobes.

Sarah looks serious as she rocks back on her haunches. I smile. Nice bum. A couple of guys have their hats on their laps. They think her bum is nice too. Flicking at the dirt in front of her with a stick, she waits for us to settle down. We press against our backpacks stuffed with clothes, rock climbing harnesses, torches, helmets, extra batteries and insect repellent. Insects. I shudder because I know what this means: at sunset, mosquitoes dive for healthy male blood. It is a massacre. During the day, it's the bush flies. Thousands of them. I ruffle through my pack. Relief — insect repellent.

Some guys pack contraband to get through camp. Fat George has junk food hidden in a side pocket. Con has the ten thick sandwiches his mother made him. Andrew is sure to have X-rated magazines shoved into the bottom of his sleeping bag. Wish Andrew and Con were here. I'd like drooling over magazines and gorging on Con's sandwiches. We'll meet up after the cave. Hope I survive until then.

Watts will have contraband for sure. Smiley-face acid on blotting paper. Easy to hide, easy to swallow a trip. Watts will have cigarettes hidden somewhere as well. I've smoked a couple of times, but kissing tastes like shit with nicotine breath. So I don't smoke. Laura smokes, but not when I'm around.

Getting caught with contraband means suspension or expulsion. Watts will never get caught. No one has the guts to say anything and the teachers are blind, or maybe just stupid. I shake my head. I don't have the guts. I look around and see Fat George. Imagine George being expelled for contraband. Stuffing his face with red jelly frogs. I laugh to myself.

Sarah instructs us about first aid. Emergency action. Calling for help. What to do with cuts, sprains, breaks, spider bites, asthma. That leer on Watts's face is disgusting. I know he's stripping her naked with his eyes — and the rest. It's not the naked part that worries me. It's the rest. When he is on dope, he just has this dumb, dazed look on his face and hangs around with the other dopeheads. It's when he's on acid that I get nervous. 'If a snake bites you, use a pressure bandage. Keep still . . .' We know all this. How many first-aid courses do you have to do? I look around. George is sweating even though it's cold. At night the temperatures go down to minus seven. Better make sure my ear lobes haven't broken off. There'll be ice in the morning for sure. In the day it will be a sweaty, dirty heat.

The fire is blazing. Waves of heat take the chill out of the air and I focus on the flickering flames. Sarah's voice is tough, but sometimes she laughs like Laura does. I look at her differently then and half listen to her. I felt bad leaving Mum to go to camp. Not that Mum said anything, but since Grandpa died she's quieter. I think it's lonely for her in Grandpa's house.

We've always lived in Grandpa's house. The photos on the mantelpiece are mainly photos of me at school, me on Santa's lap, me in my soccer team, my first day at school, me. There is one of Grandpa and Grandma on their wedding day. Grandma died when I was a baby. Stroke. I can't remember her. There is a good photo of Grandpa and Mum fishing. Mum hates taking the hook out of the fish's mouth. There is a never-to-be-talked-about photograph of Mum holding a baby in hospital. It isn't on the mantelpiece. I found it one day at the back of a drawer. (Mum cried when I showed it to her.) Mum was seventeen when she had me. My father broke her heart.

Grandpa loved camping. Not this sort of camping where you are trapped with Watts and the long drop. Camping where you can investigate a waterfall, lie under stars, smell the eucalyptus, or just think. Grandpa always wore a checked flannel shirt and I always wore a checked flannel shirt. He was as good as Seaten at making a fire and we'd push marshmallows onto bush sticks and watch them go black in the flames. Inside they were white, sweet, runny. Grandpa told me stories around the fire.

Sarah's voice penetrates my daze. 'Safety is essential.' She pulls back her brown hair. It's short and bounces into place when she lets it go. She holds up a helmet. 'This helmet will protect you against falling rocks, but the real protection is each other.' Sarah has got to be kidding. I glance at George, who has this terrified look on his face, then at Watts. Watts hates Fat George. Maybe hate is the wrong word. Watts plays with him like he would play with a fat grub. Rolling the jelly white layers around and around with a stick, prodding the underbelly, squashing a bit here and a bit there with his metal-tipped boots.

Sarah walks over to the crates that had been dragged from the coach. 'When I give you the instruction, everyone take one thing from these crates. Whatever you take, it is your responsibility, even when another bivvy group is using it. If you lose it, then you pay for it. Remember that we need everything in these crates to make the expedition work.' She tips spades, climbing ropes, bottles of disinfectant, one-litre water containers, washing-up bowls, condiment jars, iodine and other things onto a plastic ground sheet. 'Take something now.'

There is a rumble as everyone charges for the gear. I dive for the nailbrushes. Watts grabs a bottle of spices. Weedy Spano picks up the bottle of iodine. Everyone gets something, even Seaten. He's carrying a washing-up bowl. I start laughing. George is holding the dixie. The 30-litre steel cooking pot is nearly as big as his stomach and just as heavy. It won't fit into his backpack and he can't exactly jam it into his side pocket with the red jelly frogs. George and the dixie. Poor Fat George.

'Get into your bivvy groups,' Sarah calls out. 'Four groups of four.' I glance at Watts and his bivvy group. Bennie has been shoved into it by Seaten. I'm glad I'm not Bennie. There will be drugs and drinking tonight. I want to be as far away from them as possible.

George is standing next to me with his huge dixie. Seaten points to George. 'You're with Knox.' Seaten hates me.

Peter Jones looks at me. We nod at each other. He's in our bivvy. He slings his backpack over one shoulder and grabs his sleeping bag. Spano is standing by himself. Seaten points him in our direction. I groan.

Sarah is still organising 'You've been at camp before. You know the duties. Cooking, health, fire and water. There are mapping and food drop responsibilities for the expedition as well. Compasses, maps, foodstuffs are over there. Get on with it.' She stands with her hands on her hips. 'We'll see who are men around here.' She laughs as if it's a private joke. Then she walks off in her heavy boots to set up her campsite.

Watts shouts, 'We're doing fire.'

There are moans from everyone because Seaten has done it already. That means Watts's bivvy group gets out of work tonight. No one argues, because Watts will smash their head in and there is no escape from him here.

Spano is a bloody idiot and yells out, 'We're water.' Jones belts him in the arm, but it's too late. Everyone is laughing.

'Right, you're water,' guys shout out.

Spano doesn't get it. He thinks he's beaten the others to it. He is an idiot. Water is the worst. No one wants water tonight. I'm bloody tired already, as well as starving. Water means we've got to take everyone's water bottles down to the stream — wherever that is — fill them all up, put the iodine into each bottle, then carry them back to camp.

Luke calls out health. I can't wait for us to be on that. I love shit. As if. You get to dig the toilet and shove dirt on top when we leave site. No one has to dig tonight because of the long drop. They still get to do the disinfectant bowl and nailbrush routine. No hepatitis for us. There is the garbage as well. The paper is all right. We burn that at night. We burn the cans as well so they're just black metal bits. It's the plastic garbage that stinks. Flies and maggots live inside the rotting left-over food. I hate carrying the plastic garbage, especially in the heat of the day. The environment is saved, but not us.

Cooking. The last bivvy group gets that one. The megalomaniacs love cooking. They get to control who is going to starve or not, who is going to eat crap or not. Nobody else loves cooking. Cooking means complaints and whingeing, shouting, dying, moaning. The food is disgusting. You've really got to try powdered meat to know what vomit tastes like. The guys can't cook. There is never enough food, but there is plenty of sand. Peanut butter and sand. Rice and sand. Porridge and sand. Baked beans and sand.

We're nearly organised. There are just food drops and mapping. I'm doing mapping. Jones is doing mapping too. Spano and George volunteer for the food drops. That means they'll do nothing because everyone knows they're useless. Food drops. Working out food for eight days: how much to carry now, and when and what to have in the next food drop is hard. I'd rather do mapping and eat back at home. I wish. Roast chicken, seasoned bacon stuffing, peas, baked potatoes and pumpkin, fresh grain bread and lots of butter. No, I've got to stop thinking of baked dinners. It's the way to insanity. Jones shoves my shoulder. 'Are you right?'

'Right.' Ropes, the bivvy, ground sheet. I scout for a good spot. 'Over here.'

Jones nods. Spano complains until Jones stands over him and tells him to shut up. George just makes it up the rise struggling with his dixie. I know how to put up a bivvy because of Grandpa. Jones stands like a beast looking at this flat piece of plastic. 'So what do we do with this?'

Spano may be a weed, but he is a pushy weed. He takes one corner and a rope and ties the entire bivvy to one tree, so it hangs like a wet condom. I push him aside and untie it from the tree, swearing. Spano pisses off and sits down mumbling to himself. George tries to be helpful and starts to put up one side. Jones gets everyone's gear together and puts it under the drop sheet because it is starting to drizzle. Wet gear is *the* worst.

'Move out of the way.' I grab the bivvy and lie it down flat. I point to the corners. 'It needs four anchors and a couple in the middle to tie ropes onto. Then we can start making it into a tent.' I rip a handful of grass from the ground and twist one corner of the bivvy sheet around it. Then I get a rope and tie a clove hitch knot over the grass knob. I pull it tight. 'Looks good.' I glance at Jones. 'Need to do the same to all the corners of the bivvy so there are four ropes to tie the tent down.' Jones works it out straightaway. George tries. Spano doesn't.

Jones is quick. 'Corners done. Good.' I make a couple of grass knobs in the middle of the bivvy and knot a rope round each. Six ropes. Six anchors. There are plenty of trees around. I look for two that are close together. 'Right Jones. Tie that top rope to that tree.' I tie the other top rope to the other tree. The bivvy is hanging there like a soggy sheet between the trees. 'Okay, spread it.' A dirty joke flickers into my head, but only for a second. We're getting bloody wet. 'Take a corner and tie it to a bush.'

The bivvy is up, our stuff is dry and we are wet.

Jones nods at me. 'Great.'

George thinks he did it. 'Thanks.'

Jones half smiles. Spano is still mumbling and doing nothing. Jones tells him to shut up again.

We're lucky. The drizzle stops and the stream isn't too far away. 'Come on.' Jones starts to head for the water bottles dumped on the flat. I follow him. Then George rumbles after us. Spano is sitting under the bivvy.

'Are you coming, Spano?' I yell.

'Later. I don't like this,' he whines.

'You're the one who said we'd do water.' George's face is explosive red.

'I'm cold. It's wet,' Spano mumbles.

'Let's move. We'll get Spano later,' Jones shouts, racing towards the flat. 'If we don't go for the water, we won't get to mapping, then we don't eat and we'll be stuffed.'

Iodine. I forgot. I race back to get it from Spano's backpack.

'Don't throw my stuff out, Knox.' He gets up to stop me. That's like a mosquito trying to stop an elephant. It's irritating, except an elephant can just squash a mosquito. I chuck everything out of Spano's bag into the rain. The mosquito grabs my arm. I flick Spano off. It's easy. I've always been a big guy, but it's only this year that I've realised what big means. Not like Fat George with his blubbery stomach, but strong. Strong enough for anyone to think twice before they have a go at me. I don't like fighting, but I'll defend myself these days. I learnt that from Grandpa. He fought in the war over Germany as an Air Force gunner.

Mum always told me to turn the other cheek; maybe because she's female, maybe because she's kind. Except I'm not Jesus. And look what happened to him. After the war, my Grandpa didn't believe much in religion. 'There is a Creator,' he'd say. He liked the Old Testament. An eye for an eye, a tooth for a tooth. I don't want to fight, but I will.

'Found it.' I hold up the iodine.

CHAPTER 3

Even though George is shivering and slow, he's fast enough when it comes to food. He's at the front of the line. A ladle full of minced meat, mushrooms, tomatoes slosh into his yellow plastic bowl. He rips a chunk of bread from an uncut loaf. Minced meat, tomatoes, bread and sand. But it's fresh. It's the only fresh food we'll have until the next food drop. On the last camp we tried carrying unrefrigerated meat for a day in the heat. The maggots were happy, but we didn't want to eat their leftovers. George is looking at the minced meat and vegetables. Only one bowl of food. He's going to lose weight unless he has another supply of red jelly frogs hidden somewhere.

Day One and I'm so tired, cold and hungry that the hot mince stew tastes okay. I shovel it in, then rub my bread against the sides of the bowl before stuffing the bread into my mouth. It takes the edge off my hunger and pushes heat inside me. I can actually feel my toes defrosting. I look around. Luke is pumping energy. He's always on the move, not like Bennie. Bennie is leaning over his pack. He's not eating. He'll get colder for sure. Rain is dribbling down his anorak. I don't know Bennie that well, or not at all really. He's into music. I heard him play the trumpet in a band at school. I wonder if all Chinese are into trumpets? Not a bad singer as well, especially compared to me. I sing in the shower. Beer songs. Mum gave me my beer song CD.

I elbow Bennie. 'Hey, it's not too bad. The stew.' Bennie squints at me. I drag myself up and take his empty plastic bowl with me. I bring back some stew. 'It's hot.' Bennie rubs the drizzle from his face, looks up at me, then digs his spoon into his bowl.

I have to admit Seaten's fire is good. Even though the wood is wet, it is still burning. I rub my hands in front of the flames. Spano has ferreted his way into the best spot. His clothes already look drier.

Sarah spreads the map over the ground, pointing out destination points. Seaten butts in as she talks — 'You have to get up early.' 'Work out what route to take.' 'How long?' 'Camp near water.' 'Bag your dry clothes.' Turning her head slightly towards Seaten, Sarah's sharp white teeth cut him off like sliced salami. 'That's their decision, not yours.'

Seaten hesitates. I look at Sarah with her short brown hair tied back into a knot and her big boots. It feels strange watching Seaten hesitating. Seaten with his red, freckly arms shoving Fat George at me. Seaten ordering the farting coach up the mountain track. Seaten making Mum cry. Seaten doesn't interrupt again, even though Sarah is only a girl with tennis ball tits.

Sarah points to the river on the map. 'Canoes have been left here for the expedition to get down the river. You have to end up over there.'

'We won't have time to canoe there. What about the mountain in between the bends?' Jones rubs the blond stubble on his chin.

'You'll have to portage over the mountain.'

Moaning. Groaning. Everyone knows what carrying a canoe with all our gear up a mountain means. Sarah submerges a laugh. 'I see you've portaged before.' She leans over the map, tracing the route with her fingers. Abseiling cliffs, trekking wilderness, the subterranean caves. Drips trickle under my shirt, webbing shivers into the small of my back. I hack a cough. There was talk at school about caves other groups have gone down. Caves like in folklore with wicked wizards and snarly snakes. There was that cave; the rabbit-hole gap; that underground shaft; the black-ice river. From the corner of my eye, I watch George scraping the dixie clean and Spano heading for the bivvy. From the corner of my eye, I cringe at fingers and boots wedged in rock and mud.

'I'll leave the expedition planning up to you. You had better not take us the wrong way,' Sarah teases. She stands up, brushes muddy dirt from her long johns. Seaten stands up and brushes muddy dirt from his khaki shorts. I watch as he follows her.

'I'd like to take her any way,' Watts smirks.

'Shut up, Watts,' Jones slings back at him.

'You want her, do you?' He doesn't wait for an answer. Watts is laughing as he heads off with his mates towards the long drop track, except he's not going to the long drop. Ever since we set up camp he has been edgy — kicking dirt, punching guys in the arm, giving George a hard time, hanging out for something. He'd better not be bombed out tomorrow morning. We've got a lot of ground to cover. I shudder. Watts. I want to punch him out one day.

'Smart-arse,' Jones glares at Watts.

'Yeah.' I scratch the short stubble on my head, then scratch my face. Not much growth there, but with no showers, no shaving, I might get some face fuzz. Jones already has some fuzz.

Jones is Viking-blond. He rarely has an expression on his face. Sometimes I think he's made of stone. Not the ordinary stone you see on the road mixed with the bitumen, but hard, clear quartz. Everyone wants him on their team. He is straight, does the right thing; if you don't cross him, that is.

'What about being the navigator, Jones?' I hand him the compass. Navigator is a rough job. Make a mistake and the expedition could end up on the wrong side of the river, or nowhere near the food drop, or diving off the end of a cliff. Make a mistake and you could get punched out.

He stands silently for a while, watching Watts disappear into the dark. Then he turns to look at guys drying their shirts in front of the fire, Fat George frothing with the effort of cleaning the dixie. 'Sure.' Jones puts the compass in his jacket.

Planning is complicated. We have to work out more than directions and crossing rivers. How much can the guys in our expedition take? George is slow. Spano whines. Luke is rugged. Watts is a wild card. We work out strategies. 'There's a track there, alongside the creek. It'd be good to have water when it gets hot in the middle of the day. Give slow guys a chance to cool down and catch up.'

Jones agrees.

We wrangle over mountain passes and creeks. Some of the guys are like Luke: they're that fit they could carry Fat George on their backs and still make it, but George is going to find it tough. I glance at our bivvy. There is no movement. Spano is probably asleep. I don't hate Spano because he's not worth hating.

'We'd better start early tomorrow?'

I nod. 'We need to cover as much ground as we can while we're not that tired.'

'Right.'

We are going to be exhausted by the end of the week: getting to food drops on time, negotiating wilderness tracks, finding level campsites, surviving freezing nights, trekking for water. Then there is the cave. They say there are tiger snakes and stinking bats in there. And down the shaft, there's darkness like dying. Jones shrugs it off. It's eleven by the time we work out the route, where food has to be dropped, the estimated times to get to points.

'Four a.m. start tomorrow morning,' we yell as we head back to our tents.

There's yelling back — 'What bloody fool organised that?' 'Just try and get me up then.' 'You'll get crap for breakfast.' 'So what's new?' 'Was that a snake crawling up your arse?' 'Very funny.'

'Shut up and get to sleep,' Seaten's voice booms out, slashing across the voices.

'Right, sir.' 'Yeah, love sleeping on rocks.' 'Great, it's raining again.'

'Shut up,' Seaten yells out again.

Jones smiles at the comments as we climb the hill to our site. George is still awake with the dixie beside him. His waterproof jacket is zipped right up to his neck and his red and blue beanie is pulled down to his eyebrows. He's halfway into the bivvy trying to squeeze in next to Spano, who is in his sleeping bag pretending to be asleep. Spano is only small, but he has spread himself right across the middle of the bivvy.

'Move Spano.' Jones kicks him.

Spano rolls onto his side and starts to answer back, then has second thoughts. Jones towers over the weed. Spano's instinct for survival must be turned on. He shuffles to the edge of the ground sheet. George slots in beside him, although not really 'slots'; maybe slugs in beside him with his dixie is more like it.

'Get that dixie out of here,' Jones rumbles.

'But if someone takes it, there's no cooking pot. It's our only cooking pot.'

'Don't be so bloody stupid. Who'd want to steal the dixie?' I thump George.

'The dixie is out of here.' Jones isn't interested in talking about it any more.

George carefully pushes the clean dixie into the drizzle. I slide into my bag next to him, then Jones gets into his bag. Four peas in a pod. It is freezing. Snow peas. My balls are shrivelled in their pod. I check to see if they are still there. It's okay, they're there. I pull my beanie over my eyes, my nose, mouth, right down to my neck. It has slits for my eyes like a balaclava. I look like Bennie. I want to make a joke, then have second thoughts. Poor Bennie.

My sleeping-bagged feet are sticking out of the bivvy in the rain. Jones's feet are sticking out further. George and Spano's feet are not. Five hours before we have to get up and I need sleep. I can hear faint voices coming from the bush. Probably Watts. Probably pissed or doped.

Stuff that bastard. I want Laura. Hmm, Laura. Sleep. My eyes are leaden. Laura has such beautiful breasts and I'm touching them. Soft skin, cherry nipples . . . What's in my ear? Something is in my ear. I shake my head.

Laura.

I shake my head again but it won't go away. I force my eyes open and stare right into George's big, ugly face. Muffled whimpering is coming out of him.

I belt into his arm with my index knuckle. It'll give him a dead arm for sure. 'Shut up, George.'

There are stammering gasps, then a pathetic moan. He's holding his arm. I don't care. Who asked him to be in our bivvy? George is a bloody idiot. I burrow deeper into my sleeping bag, close my eyes. Laura. Tits. Round, soft. The whimpering starts again. Whimper, whimper, sniffle. It's like a tap dripping on my head. Drip, drip, drip. Laura disappears. I'll rip off George's arm in a minute. 'What's wrong, George?'

'Nothing.'

'Good, then shut up.'

'Why don't you shut up, Knox?'

'I don't have to. You're the one who's a snivelling baby. Now, get to sleep or camp over the edge of a cliff or something. Maybe you'll fall off.'

'You're a shit.'

'So I'm a shit. Are you going to shut up?'

Silence. Good. Then George starts hiccupping. Hiccups, snorts, hiccups. I shove George hard. Louder hiccups. 'Right. It's like this. I want sleep. I need sleep. So tell me what's wrong, NOW.' I grab his fat arm. 'Talk or die.'

Hiccups.

'I said talk or I'll twist this arm right off.'

'You're breaking it. Stop it. Stop.' I twist his arm harder. Harder. 'All right, all right. I'll talk,' he splutters. 'I hate it here.'

'So? Unless you're Luke who thinks he's superman or Seaten, who doesn't?'

'Seaten hates me.'

'He hates everyone. Is that it?' I shuffle deeper into my sleeping bag. It's bloody freezing. 'Go to sleep.'

George is wide awake and definitely not silent. He's snorting like a bull in my ear. I grit my teeth. 'So is there anything else, George?'

His breath is heavy. He stammers. 'Watts is going to kill me. I know it.'

'Watts? He won't kill you. I will.'

George shakes his head, muttering some pathetic noises.

I look into George's bloodshot eyes and know that his snivelling is going to go on all night if I don't do something. 'I won't let him kill you. All right? Now, stop moaning. Go to sleep.'

George shivers. 'He's going to drown me in the black ice river in the cave,' he whispers. 'I'll be frozen and dead. Or . . .'

'Or nothing.' I've got to sleep. 'No one is going to get you. Okay?'

George looks at me with panicked eyes. He blinks hard. I can smell his fear. I know Watts is a real bastard. I've seen it. I look at George holding his arm. He'll get a bruise where I knuckled him. 'You'll be with me in the cave, right?'

Pressing his lips together, he nods like a string-puppet, but George isn't a puppet and I can see he's afraid. 'Watts will have to get past me first, right.' My throat tightens. George closes his eyes, then opens them. 'I promise. I won't let him get near you. It'll be okay.' There are some whimpers, but I don't knuckle him again. I wait a few minutes. George hiccups a couple of more times, opens his eyes, sees me staring at him, closes his eyes. 'Sleep, George.'

Then George is snoring, that heavy, grunting snore of someone trying to find air through a dark underground passage. I look over at Spano who is wheezing. Jones is silent. There are noises — Watts and his mates rumbling back to their bivvy. Tripping. I wonder where Bennie is. There are other sounds — the shrieking of birds, possums up trees, wild dogs. They are vicious those dogs, feral. People say they take chickens, small lambs, even babies if you are not looking. Rip out their throats. A shiver tears down my spine. My eyelids flicker at the sounds of bush shrieking, then close into half-dreams and memory. Camping with Grandpa. It was a happy day. Just us. Then the four of them appeared.

We were walking back from the river, very satisfied with ourselves. We had caught three trout and dinner looked as if it was going to be great. Grandpa had his fishing rod over his shoulder and I was holding the fishing box and bucket with the trout. We had seen dogs in the area, so when we set up camp we had been careful to move away from their territory.

'Don't trespass,' Grandpa said.

But these were looking for trouble. They found us walking back and started to follow, tagging us with low growls.

'Grandpa,' I whispered.

Grandpa looked back at them. 'It's all right, Sam.'

I saw from the periphery of my eye their snarls, the black undersides of their lips, their yellow fangs, their butcher tongues.

'Walk next to me,' Grandpa said quietly. 'Not too fast.'

I wanted to run. I knew they'd get me if I ran, but that was what I wanted to do. I started to walk faster. They did too. Then they began to gain on us, worrying the bush, snarling, spitting out growls. I walked faster. They moved more quickly. I could smell their saliva. Suddenly Grandpa clenched my arm, forcing me to stop. I could hardly breathe. He turned around. I turned around after him.

Snarling drool dripped like blood. They were going to rip out our throats for sure. I was cold, frozen, breathing razor blades. I looked at Grandpa. We had nothing to fight with. He stared into their eyes and they stared back, still edging forward. Then Grandpa started. I'd never heard him swear like that before, but he swore then with angry frightening, obscenities, spitting out 'bloody bastards', 'crap dogs', 'bloody animals', 'killing shits'.

I couldn't move. The ferals stopped edging towards us, unsure of whom this ferocious Grandpa was in his checked flannel shirt. He took out his flimsy fishing rod, whipping it at the dogs, then he charged them, my Grandpa with his white hair and heavy-rimmed glasses.

They stopped snarling, unsure, then they turned, running like cowards into the scrub.

I learnt something that day.

I look at my watch. Nearly midnight. I've got to stop thinking, get some sleep. I hate getting up in the dark, and it will be freezing in the morning. I have to stop thinking. George is snoring beside me. It's better than his whimpering. I'm so tired and there is health tomorrow morning ... Cooking the dinner ... I'm not carrying the plastic garbage ... six hours of rotting food on my back ... no way ... I've got to sleep ... Laura.

CHAPTER 4

Last night I was so exhausted that, finally, nothing, not even farting Spano, the rocky ground, howling mongrels, George's snoring, or Laura's body could keep me conscious. The last thing I heard was noise coming from Watts and his mates.

Watts. That bastard. He goes for anyone who he thinks is weaker. He was that manic at the last Rave party, he crossed the line. Some of it was speed, but not the rest. It's okay to be insane at Raves. Andrew is. But it's not okay to be Watts insane.

At that last Rave the band jackhammered techno music. Everyone was thumping, jumping. The mosh pit was really pumping when a couple of girls went for it and jumped into the pit, crowd surfing right over the top of us. They screamed when they got pressed against the security fence. Guards pulled them out of it. Andrew jumped in after them. He couldn't care less about being crushed to death as long as there are girls with him. His brain has become a sex pit. He's driving us crazy. He has got to get more than a one-night stand. He needs a girlfriend or we're going to have to exterminate him. But the Rave was bad. Watts was bad.

I have to get up. It is freezing, but at least it has stopped raining. It is going to be a long trek today. Shivering. This isn't what camping is about. Only an idiot would be out in this bloody weather. Is it really morning? It's cold, dark and I want breakfast. Hot porridge, warm milk, melted butter, brown sugar. No, stop, stop. Just as long as there isn't too much sand in the baked beans, it'll be fine. Got to get up. I roll onto my side, but there is something in the way. George. He is sitting up like a right angle, with a bulge under his neck finishing at his stomach. His face is puffy and pale. 'Are you all right?'

George shakes his head and points to his boots.

'You're an idiot. You have to sleep with your shoes on inside your sleeping bag.' George's boots are solid ice. I slept with my shoes on last night and I wriggle my toes. My feet are still warm, but my socks have a definite smell. War zone, gas mask country. Eight days without washing my socks could be the real 'challenge' for this camp. It's my secret weapon. Attack me and I'll shoot my socks at the enemy. They'll beg for mercy.

'I can't get the laces undone.'

I laugh at George fiddling with his shoes. In the torchlight, his stubby fingers look like thick white sausages.

'What's so funny?'

'Nothing.' I whack his sleeping bag. 'Stick your shoes in your sleeping bag for a couple of minutes. It'll still be hot inside. That'll defrost them enough to get the laces loose. Put your hands in too.'

There are torches flickering from other tents at Base Camp. The fire detail must be up already. The fire is raging and I'm dying for a piss.

'Four-thirty. We're late.' Jones stretches out like a taut spring. 'Better pack up.' A rumbling fart whispers out of Spano's green ultra-light sleeping bag. He has been showing off about his sleeping bag for weeks, except no one cares. My sleeping bag is old and heavy, but I like it. Grandpa gave it to me.

Spano is still rolled inside his bag like a lump of manure. 'Get up, Spano,' Jones orders. Spano doesn't move. Jones growls, 'Get up.' The loser still doesn't move. George and I stop to watch. Jones has grit in his voice. 'Get up, Spano. Now.'

No movement. Spano must want to die. Jones hovers over the bivvy for a second, then yanks the two knots holding the wet bivvy up. It has been raining all night and no one is in a good mood. He yanks it seriously this time, burying Spano under it. There is silence. Nothing, then the lump under the plastic sheeting starts to snivel, making pathetic moaning sounds that develop into a whine. 'Stop it, you bums. Leave me alone. It's unfair ... you rotten shits ... unfair.' The lump shuffles in its tub but still doesn't get up. George and I shake our heads at each other, then look at Jones. He nods directions.

George has his boots on now and his sausage fingers are thawed pink. He pushes the dixie to safety, then grabs one end of the ground sheet, untying it from a bush. Jones grabs the other end and I yank the side, releasing the last two corners. With one enormous shove we pull the sheet from under Spano. From the collapsed bivvy, a long squealing sound like a castrated pig slashes through the freezing dark air. A few torches flash up towards us before flickering back to their sites. Spano has already started to roll, gathering speed, turning around and around like a torpedoed cucumber. He tumbles past the dixie, down the hill, oinking over rocks and branches, sloshing into this great sty of mud.

'Awake now?' Jones yells out.

We fall over each other laughing until I have to crawl out of the pack of bodies. I really need a piss. Grabbing my torch, I shove past George who is doubled over and grunting laughs. 'Have to go.' I head off to the long drop still laughing, when I trip over a fallen branch. Got to be careful. It won't be light for a while. I flash my torch to navigate the long drop track because I know the dangers of hidden piles of shit. The torch triangles light into the bush. I squint, stop laughing and head into shadows. Spano's ferret-like face flares into my mind. I don't get Spano. Whingeing, wheedling his way out of everything. He's got so much. He doesn't need to work at Pizza Palace. He's got a father too. What's wrong with him? I shake my head, then pound my arms so that my circulation keeps going. How far is the long drop?

The muffled voices at Base Camp have faded away and there is only rustling leaves, forest howls, crunching of rocks under my boots. Those shadows at the end of my torchlight are starting to look real. Zigzag prickles shiver down my spine. I check the torch. Bulb, batteries are working. I've had nightmares of batteries failing at the crucial moment on the long drop. There I am with my bum hanging over it, falling in, drowned in maggots. I cringe. What's that? A snake? That's all I need. I'm not walking any further. No one is around. Seaten and Sarah are probably drinking coffee in front of the campfire. I won't get caught.

Detour. I head for the ghost gums. At least I can see

them at night. They look like dead men's skeletons. There is some scrub near them. Got to be quick. I don't want my dick to freeze and snap off. It wouldn't be much fun watching late-night movies without it. Take a breath. Right, another breath. Fast. Drop my trousers, find my fly, pull out my dick. It is bloody freezing. Come on, don't get frozen. Relief. My bladder was going to explode thanks to Spano. Spano is a pathetic weed and ... what's that? Something is moving. Wild pigs? No, no. Voices. Is that Robbo, Watts's mate? Pull up my pants. They're halfway up. Watts. No. Don't panic. Quiet, quiet. I switch off my torch.

'You'd better keep your mouth shut. Right, Robbo,' Watts's voice grates. My trousers are sliding down my legs, but I am not moving.

'Yeah, but at the Rave, people saw it happen.'

'What? What did they see? Nothing.' Watts isn't on speed. There is no laughing, no manic energy, just a serrated rumble.

No answer. My legs are ice.

'Nothing ... happened ... Robbo.' His words truncate into long pauses. 'She hasn't said anything.' Silence. 'She won't say anything.' Silence. 'So nothing happened. Right?' Thump. Another thump. 'Right?'

'Yeah, right, Watts. Nothing happened.'

The voices disappear. My heart pounds. Are they gone? I wait. I can't feel my legs any more. I'm not moving. My trousers are cold, my balls shrunk, my dick hidden inside foreskin. The Rave. That bloody Rave. Watts is lying. Something happened that night. Something.

* * *

He was drenched, dripping sweat. 'Raving at the Rave,' I joked, nodding my head in Watts's direction. Andrew laughed before heading for the girls in the corner. Watts looked like he was heading for me. He shoved past Robbo and I started to shove away. I didn't feel like dealing with that psycho tonight. He thought he was the Mafia trying to extort free pizzas from me. Great way to lose my job or go broke.

'Hey, Knox.' His voice was hoarse.

I moved faster, elbowing through the thumping crowd. 'Get out of the way, guys.'

'Pizza puke, where are you going? Hey, I'm talking to you.' His eyes were like cracked walnuts. Had to keep moving. Robbo was behind him. 'Stop, pizza puke.' He was starting to seriously ram into kids. The crowd began parting like the Red Sea, except I wasn't Moses. The floodwaters were going to crash right over me. Watts was tracking me now. Sweat bubbled down the side of my face. I glanced back at him. It was the ferals in for the kill. My stomach wrenched into knots. Got to think. Think. Strategy. Where was Andrew? I looked around. Come on, Andrew. I couldn't see him. Watts was gaining. Got to move. Where? No gaps to move. Nowhere to run. I wanted to run. I tightened my fists into iron, breathed slowly and surveyed the room. There was plenty of off-your-face dancing, sweat, beer and no friends. Trapped. Watts had me. I stopped dead still and faced him.

'Hey, Knox.' The voice was familiar. 'Over here.' Watts looked around. I looked around. Andrew was shouting, pushing his way towards me with five girls behind him. 'Too many even for me,' he laughed. They were giggling. Watts was interested. One girl was drunk, Annie. She looked different to when I meet her at the bus stop. She's always neat at the bus stop. Always wears her hair tied up in a high ponytail. Not tonight. Her hair was tangled like bleached spaghetti. Watts wasn't interested in my pizzas any more. He was after the girls.

* * *

I saw something that night, in the Men's toilets. Annie was there. She shouldn't have been there. Not there, all bleached spaghetti matted between urinals, and grunting. No, she shouldn't have been there.

Voices disappearing. Is Watts gone? The numbness of my legs is becoming pain. I rub them, trying to force blood to move down into my feet. I rub my butt, dragging my trousers up. No voices. Move. Focus, try to think. Get back to camp. Get back. They are gone. Watts is gone. Breathing shallowly, I slowly grope around, switch on my torch and start to make my way between the trees towards the long drop track. The track. The rough stones and kicked dirt are a relief as I walk along it. I should have done more at that Rave. Then I start to jog … run … race. My blood is circulating again, pounding into my hands and feet. I grab my balls making sure they're still there, then I race like a sprinter letting dirt and rocks fly behind me in an aftermath of dust.

I see it. Base Camp. The first morning light ricochets off pots and tins. I never thought I'd be glad to see Base Camp. The sun arrows through the trees, targeting Seaten's red hair. I was right. He's chatting up Sarah in front of the fire. Steam is coming from his metal mug, or is that from his ears? It's the hot air rushing through his head. But I'm still glad to see him.

I see Watts and Robbo fossicking in their bags, checking to see if anyone has stolen something. As if anyone would be so stupid? I head into camp from another direction. Tents are packed, the area cleared, torches off. There is George and the dixie. I call out, 'What's cooking?'

He looks around, sees me. His big face is red with the heat of the fire. He answers seriously. 'Baked beans.'

'You're kidding.' I shake my head. 'Baked beans and sand.'

George's eyebrows crinkle into disappointment.

'Only kidding.' If George only knew how good it is to see him and his dixie and the baked beans mixed with sand.

Spano is stuffing himself with the beans. There will be a lot of farting tonight. I don't care. I rummage through my bag. Someone has packed it. I take out my plastic bowl and walk toward the fire. There are a few smart-arse comments — 'Fall down the long drop, did you?' 'Wanking off behind a bush, were you?' There are sniggers, laughing.

George slops beans into the bowl. No brown sugar, no butter, no real sauce. Tomato glug sprinkled with lumps, jagged bits and, yes, sand.

I slump next to Jones. 'Who packed my gear?'

'I did. You must have been storing a big piss. You were gone quite a while.'

I gulp down the beans.

Jones watches me for a minute. 'I was going to look for you.'

He wants an answer. I want to tell him, but I can't. 'Thanks. Sorry about not helping pack. I'll make it up.'

He waits, nearly says something, then nods. 'Okay.'

Spano has finished his beans and is sulking. 'I hate this. This is so unfair. I want to go home.'

Jones doesn't look up from his bowl. George stops with his ladle in his hand and I look at Spano. 'Shut up,' we all yell at him.

CHAPTER 5

Jones holds the compass. I look at it, then into the wilderness with its boulders, ferns, the gnarled roots of coachwood and sassafras. The camp is clear except for the remnants of burnt logs and the blackened fireplace. 'Ready,' Jones commands. Grumbles, laughing, jokes, surrender. Seven days. Seven days without home, Mum, late-night movies, Laura. Backpacks are slung over shoulders. George, Seaten, Luke, even Spano are ready. No choice. I look at Spano. He's been relentless, complaining to everyone that his backpack is too heavy for him. It's pathetic. Spano may be thin, but he can run fast. Really fast. He's in the school athletics team. I didn't make it. Spano is whingeing again. 'Someone's going to stuff your backpack up your nose, Spano,' I yell.

Jones ignores him. 'Let's go.' He signals that we're moving.

It's not as cold now. My fingers have defrosted and my feet are moving. Jones folds the map and slots it into his jacket. I take the compass. He nods at me as we head into undergrowth. The advance is uneven at first until we assess the terrain, find our pace. Slowly we fall into a regular rhythm as we climb over collapsed trees, force ferns apart, trek through low bush, avoid bush ant hills. Ant hills. Not the pathetic ant hills of backyard gardens, but eruptions of lava-like fortresses. Real ant hills. I laugh. I remember being attacked as a kid, wearing worn-out joggers torn by kicking balls and climbing rocks. My feet were swollen with red throbbing. Grandpa saved me, shoving ants away with his bare hands, dragging my joggers off, flooding my feet with methylated spirits. He carried me on his back to the campsite, through the bush, stomping furiously on those bull ants. After that I always wore heavy leather walking boots in the bush.

The pace is determined as Jones strides on. I stride beside him, my pulse quickening, my breath heavier. His eyes focus ahead, only squinting to the sides when a lizard rustles the undergrowth or there is a call from one of the troop behind us. Single-minded. Maybe that's what makes him good as the captain of the First Fifteen Rugby team. The trouble is that we aren't all as fast, as athletic or as determined as he is. He doesn't even feel the weight of his backpack. Jones needs to understand that George and Spano and Bennie aren't the stuff of the First Fifteen Rugby. I have to slow him down. I have to distract him if we're going to make it. Rugby. I ask about the football season. He answers monosyllabically until I get under his skin about tough scrums, metal studded tips, big kicks, a try, a field goal. He shows me plays, moves, slowing down as he kicks a phantom ball. Jones has this control, this arctic bear strength. Seaten admires him. I look back at Seaten. His face is focussed on the trek.

In summer Seaten coaches the basketball team. In winter, it's football. I play soccer. Not Seaten's favourite sport. I'm goalie for the 'Mighty D's'. No one wants to be goalkeeper. Too much stress. Everyone shouts at you not to let the ball through. I've got it worked out. I follow the striker's eyes. Ignore where he places the ball. I just watch his eyes. That's where he's going to kick. My guts are in my throat. The soccer boot smashes into the ball and I dive for it, sliding across mud, ripping my knees, throttling through the air. Adrenaline is pumping, guys screaming, the coach running along the sidelines. 'Knox, move.' 'Knox. Knox. Knox.' I've saved a lot of goals, won a few games, made great mates, played as a team. Seaten doesn't admire my soccer, but it's not about that for me.

I crunch a branch that swings back, whipping my arm. It leaves a sting. I stare at the ground. Even though the rise is slow, my legs are getting tired. I feel my calf muscles spasm. It's already hot. I glance at Jones. No, he isn't tired, striding forward like he's at a football training session. I think he likes testing himself. He wants a struggle so that he can overcome it. Is that what heroes are made of? I snigger. I'm no hero. If I could, I'd turn around and go home. Baked dinners. Laura, Mum.

I swallow a mouthful of iodine water and look back. Some of the line is struggling even with my slow-down manoeuvres. George's dixie flashes silver from between the trees. I can just see Sarah with Spano. My backpack is lead, digging into my shoulders. I jerk it around. That's better. Flies scatter everywhere. There is a blanket of flies on Jones's back. I grab a handful from his shirt and throw them at him. He laughs, but not too loudly because guys have been known to swallow one or two.

Jones stops to look back. I stop, too. Looking ahead we can't see anything much except trees. If we are going in circles . . . no. No. I squint at the compass. 'The river is over that crest. Another hour, that's all. Then we can break for lunch.'

We wait for the stragglers. Watts throws his backpack on the ground. 'What are we stopping for?' Watts isn't in a good mood. Post-hangover hate. 'It's that bloody Fat George, isn't it? Where is the fat slug?'

No one answers. What is wrong with Watts? His family seems okay. His sister is normal. Was he born on the wrong side of the moon or something? His mother always looks sort of amazed that she produced Watts. Maybe he's a throwback to Hitler, or Attila the Hun, whoever is worse. Or maybe his brain is just fried from too many drugs?

I look around for George. His dixie glints in the distance. I nudge Jones. 'What do you think? Is George lost?'

'Yeah, could be.' Jones's Viking features are chiselled hard as he glares at Spano. 'But look who isn't?'

Spano's whining has worked. He is carrying nothing, not the garbage, not his backpack, not even his super-light sleeping bag.

'How'd you manage it, Spano?' I grunt at him.

'It's not like that. I hurt my ankle. It's probably sprained, maybe even broken.'

'Sure.'

'Sarah said I couldn't carry anything. To be safe.'

'Safe?' I watch Watts grinding his metal tips into the ground.

'You're safe,' I sneer as I look at Bennie struggling with Spano's extra load.

'There'll be water in an hour or so,' Jones calls out, 'at the river.' Guys start pouring surplus water over their heads, but still leave enough for emergencies. They'll refill at the river. Spano sits on a boulder by himself. He's getting the isolation treatment. He must be really suffering. No one to whinge to.

I drop my sleeping bag and gear. 'Jones, can we stop here for a while? It's George. Got to find him.'

Jones nods.

Smart-arse comments make me laugh as I go the wrong way. 'Haven't walked enough, Knox?' 'Why don't you jog back to base.' 'Bring us back some hamburgers.'

Seaten stops me. 'Where are you going, Knox?'

'Got to get George.'

He raises his eyebrows, then waves me on as if I need his permission. I feel his stare driving into my back. I refuse to turn around.

George is an idiot, a bloody idiot. He's probably sitting on a rock stuffing red jelly frogs in his mouth. My legs hurt. I've got to be crazy doing this, but then I promised him. A promise is a promise. Grandpa always told me, keep a promise because you have to live with yourself. 'Grandpa.' I get a catch in my throat when I say his name. It has been six months since he died. Six months. It feels like forever and yesterday.

The doctor told Mum in the hospital. 'The cancer in his brain is pressing on his speech centre.' He looked at the floor as he spoke, worrying the bottom of his lip with his teeth. 'He can't walk or talk or eat.'

I smiled at the doctor because he didn't know Grandpa. Grandpa could do anything. Anything. I knew Grandpa would speak when he was ready. Grandpa was a carpenter. His workshop was amazing, with ordered shelves of hammers, nails, wood glue, drills of all shapes and sizes. I helped him repair furniture and make cabinets on the weekends and sometimes after school.

When I was six years old, there was this one special project that he wouldn't let me help him with. 'Stay in the kitchen, Sam,' he'd say. 'Help your mother.' I didn't want to help my mother and would press my nose against the wire mesh on the back flyscreen door. Mum laughed when I turned towards her because my face would be a patchwork of dents and indentations like the mesh. I hated her laughing at me and stormed out of the kitchen. Grandpa told me that I had to learn to wait because everything doesn't come easily or straightaway. Grandpa said that if I had a bad temper, that I'd have to wait longer. I waited every night. For two weeks Grandpa hammered and sawed in his workshop and then one day he stopped. 'Sam, come here,' he called to me through the wire mesh door. I followed him into the workshop.

I couldn't speak and stood staring at the soft brown leather saddle with my name carved into it. The mane and tail were gold and the reins were red. Its brown eyes seemed to know me. My rocking horse is battered now through years of riding and kids crawling on its back. I wanted to repair it after Grandpa died. It's just that I couldn't go into the workshop to get the hammers and tools. I tried, but no, I couldn't go inside.

I was standing behind Mum outside Grandpa's ward when the doctor told her. The double doors were open. The floor was grey lino. There were tall double-hung wooden windows with blinds that were stuck halfway up the window frame. There were three beds on each side divided by a wide aisle. Men with drips and bandages and crooked faces lay in each bed. Grandpa's bed was nearest the door on the left side. The curtains weren't closed properly. The doctor spoke quietly. He said Grandpa had 'passed away'. I peered into the ward. A white sheet was draped over Grandpa; over his body, over his head, over his carpenter hands. He didn't have a head any more. No face, no legs, no arms, not even the drip snaking into the back of his hand. But his glasses were still on the chest of drawers next to the bed.

The doctor's words were hard to understand, even though I was listening very carefully. I really listened, but how could I hear when the doctor had ripped my guts out? I reeled back, pressing against the corridor wall, gasping for air. I didn't know you could have so much pain and live.

I didn't cry at first. Mum cried and I put my arms around her. But I couldn't . . . I didn't know how to cry then. I cried later. Every night. And I was angry and couldn't forgive Grandpa for leaving. Later, Grandpa came back to me and visited inside me. Sometimes, we talk at night. Sometimes in the day. Sometimes I reel backwards with the ache of no Grandpa beside me.

George. Where is George? The sunlight gives the eucalyptus trees a silvery shine. Sunlight flashes between the logs, ferns, rocks. I squint, looking for another flash from George's dixie. I've got to find George. The whole trek has stopped because of him. Come on. How far back are you? I start to speed up. At least it's downhill. A flash. It's got to be the dixie. That stupid dixie. Dixie and George. Haven't you heard of survival, George? The dixie is so damn big. Only an idiot would have picked it. Only an idiot would be looking for you. For God's sake, where are you, George?

The glints are stronger and I move quickly. I think it's him. I can make out the shape of the pot. George is under it. Is that George? Yes. Yes. Can he see me? No. He's bending forward like a ball of crumpled newspaper. What's he looking at? Dirt? His boots? George's frozen boots this morning were pretty funny and that insane dixie sitting on his shoulders. It makes him look like a hunchback.

George shudders in surprise when I grab his pack. I start to unhook the dixie. 'Hold still, George.' His large, round face peers at me and there is a confused look. 'George, it's Sam.' The dixie is off him. 'I ought to get a chain and drag you up the mountain.' I strap the dixie onto my back. 'You're a useless log. Maybe that's what you'd be good at, being a log. We could feed you mud and sticks.'

George starts to straighten up without the weight of the dixie, but he is still standing around half dazed. His water bottle is empty. I give him mine. He stares at the bottle for a while, then drinks.

'Come on.' He just stands there. 'Let's get moving George, or do you need me to carry you as well as the dixie? You're hopeless.'

A spark begins to flicker in George's eyes and he murmurs back, 'I am not.'

'Right, then move your arse. Or are you going to slobber behind everyone the whole camp?'

'No, and I don't slobber.'

'Sure, you do. Slobber.'

'I don't,' George mutters.

'Slobber, slobber, slobber.'

George's face goes red.

'You're a useless lump.'

'Lump?' George's eyebrows crinkle into a V-shape.

'That's what I said. Lump.'

He glares at me. 'I'm not a lump.' It takes him a while to think of a comeback. 'Who does the cooking?'

'No one since you are slacking around here and we're all starving. Have you heard of lunch?'

'Lunch. I've heard of it.' George's voice is louder. His brain is starting to work. His legs are starting to work. 'The last time you cooked, lunch was burnt garbage.'

George isn't shuffling any more even though it is uphill. He is actually getting up a bit of pace. 'Garbage? You're garbage.'

'Right, I'll show you.' George is walking faster. His feet don't drag any more and he is beginning to get his bearings. He drinks my water bottle dry.

'Sure.'

George gets into action. His sausage fingers push branches and overgrown ferns aside and his thick legs pound the rocky ground. I look at my watch. We are making good time even though the dixie is pressing into my back and sweat dribbles down my shirt.

Relief. We are close now. I whack George on the shoulder. 'They're just over that next rise.' He walks faster, but I'm getting nervous. Some of the guys are going to be edgy after waiting around. Watts will rip right into George for sure. I'm not ready for Watts. I've got to try and deflect him. If Watts sees the dixie on my back, there is no way of saving George. 'Sorry about the cooking, George. I was just joking. You're a great cook, even with all the sand.'

'What sand?' George attacks.

'Just joking, George. No sand. Do you want to carry the dixie now? Oh, don't worry, it's too heavy for you. I'll do it.' His eyebrows gather into this serious look and I want to laugh. I don't.

'Give me the dixie.'

'Right.'

We climb over the last stretch. Jones is looking out for us. He glances up at George with the dixie strapped to his back, waves, then shouts out to the group, 'Let's get moving.'

There are a few insults. 'You'd make great dog bait.' 'We should have left you for the wild pigs.' There are a few punches in the arm. George just misses out on a dead arm when a fist slams into the dixie. Watts makes a few smart-arse comments to his mates and they sneer, but they don't go over to George. Mainly because Sarah has been on the lookout. She sprints towards George. Seaten watches and Watts smirks. 'She must be into fat. I could show her a few things.' 'Yeah,' Robbo pumps his arms backwards and his hips forwards. As if he's had any.

Jones is already heading for the river and I'm feeling exhausted. I walk alongside George. Sarah looks at the dixie. 'We're going to have to share the carrying of the dixie. What do you think?'

'I can do it,' George explodes.

I nod at Sarah.

She smiles. 'I know you can George, but . . .'

CHAPTER 6

Lunch has to be quick because we have wasted too much time already. Crispbread and peanut butter. Water bottles filled. Three drops of iodine added. The river isn't a river. It is only a rocky stream, with trickling water and ragged foam. I splash my face. Its coldness is a relief from the heat of the day. Then I notice George sitting on a rock at the water's edge. It's too good an opportunity to miss. Splash.

'Hey,' George shouts as the cold spray hits him. There is a second of panic in his eyes, then he sees it's me. His eyes crinkle into a grin. He looks at me, then slams the water back and it is on. Everyone is in, except for Spano. No one is interested enough to waste a splash on him.

He doesn't get it. Thinks he's persecuted, but it's just that he isn't a mate. He never cares about anything except himself. I just want to say 'piss off' to him all the time.

Jones and Watts engage in a furious battle of attacks and charges. Watts hold Jones's face under the water, until Jones grabs Watts's arm twisting it like it's breaking. They gasp for air staring at each other, then start again. A few guys egg them on, but it's George who holds centre stage.

'Come on, George, you can do it.' 'Get Robbo.' 'George power.' 'Sumo George.'

Like a great hippo he rolls Robbo, splashing everyone including Seaten. There are cheers and yells of 'George the Great', 'Sumo the King'. Robbo struggles for air trying to call out, 'Enough.' George is having too much fun dunking Robbo, tripping him with judo moves and arm wrestling. In the end, two of us have to grab George and sit on him, otherwise he'd drown Robbo.

George squelches and bellows, then starts laughing, a contagious rumbling noise. Even Seaten catches it, laughing as he calls out, 'Had enough boys?'

Sarah's laughing as well and she shouts back, 'This girl has.' She points to her watch. 'What's happening?'

Jones looks at his watch. He motions to Watts that he has finished the war and leaves him standing with his feet apart. Watts shakes his head as he twists water from the edge of his army shirt. He smirks as though he has won something. 'We'll finish this later, Jones.'

Jones shrugs and heads for his backpack. The blond hairs on the back of his arm glisten as he wipes sweat and cold water off his face. He pulls out the compass and map from his backpack, smoothing the map flat onto the ground.

We release Fat George, who is happy hassling us. 'Needed two of you to get me down? No muscles.'

'At least my muscles aren't in my head, George.' I flick his hair.

George gives a know-all smile. 'I showed you.'

'That's right, George.' I roll my eyes, but I smile. George did show us something. He showed himself something.

A few guys slap George on the back. 'You're a legend, George.'

'In your own mind,' I say.

George gets a new name, Sumo George.

He shuffles off to get a towel and I go to help Jones. He skims a look at me as he studies the map. 'What do you think?'

I crouch beside him. 'We're behind time. We won't be at camp till dark. Maybe ten.' Walking in the early evening is good. No flies. It is cooler, easier, but later than that is different. Temperatures drop like smashed glass. Freezing. It's hard to find your way in the dark with only the moon and stars, trekking through bush with torches. George may be Sumo George, but he could get lost, and there are roaming dogs, and Watts gets aggressive with no smokes or dope.

I look around. Robbo is sizzling like burnt paper. Watts gave him a hard time about George. 'You're a dickhead. Did Fat George squash you?' Watts belted him a couple of times.

Now Seaten is aggravating him. 'What are you doing? Move.' Robbo swears under his breath as he grabs his backpack and heads after Jones. Seaten is organising, as usual. If he's trying to impress her, he hasn't worked it out. Sarah isn't impressed. She has just given up telling him that this is supposed to be our challenge, not his.

Seaten knows the wilderness like my Grandpa. Really knows it. Seaten could guide us over mountain cliffs and crocodile infested swamps in darkest Africa. I glare at him. I would never ask Seaten for help.

Jones folds the map into quarters. He stands straight, puts on his bush hat, bends his head towards me. 'Ready?'

I tug at my hat. 'Ready.'

Jones calls out, 'Let's go.' There is shuffling, picking up gear, swearing, packing the garbage. Seaten is checking that George's dixie is tied on properly.

'Don't worry about Sumo George, he can carry a horse,' Luke shouts out.

'Sumo is a bloody horse.' There are a few laughs, but it's different.

George makes a loud neighing sound. 'No one can buck me.'

'Right.'

We start walking, falling into some sort of trekking order with Watts and his pack in the middle, Spano ferreting his way between the victims who are carrying his gear, and Seaten at the back instructing Bennie about abseiling. Since Bennie doesn't say much, he's a great target for Seaten. Then it is uphill again, into rough country.

Some of us talk, complain, joke as we force our boots forward, straddling trees, crashing through scrub, pushing uphill. The sun beats a strong mid-afternoon heat that crisps and crackles fallen leaves. Our clothes dry, marking us as targets. Flies land in battalions, sucking on the sweat that trickles from under our hats. I glance back. George is dragging behind, but he is all right.

The first hour dribbles into the next, until we don't speak. It's too hard. We need all our physical energy to walk. I focus on my feet, ignoring the straps of my backpack digging into my shoulders. I force my mind to move away from the muscles cramping in my legs. A blue-tongue lizard darts for cover under red spiky banksias and undergrowth. Flashes of Grandpa paste their way between the leaves. Grandpa in shorts sitting with Mum on a log in bush like this. Mum only went camping with Grandpa because it made him happy. It was the opposite for me.

I did the Blue Mountains track with Andrew and Con. It was different to this. Three days of tough hiking, no tents, no parents, but we'd chosen to go. It didn't rain and we were friends. I got to eat Con's cabbage rolls and investigate Andrew's porn magazines. Disgusting stuff. At night we slept pretty far apart. Erotic dreams. I thought about sex with Laura in every position. She won't go all the way. We do a lot of touching but I'm hoping. I carry condoms just in case.

Poor Con doesn't get much chance to go out with girls. He is dying to make it with a girl, but he's always at Greek family parties or has to go out with cousins. I've never known anyone with so many cousins. I have a few distant relatives but I hardly ever see them. Con has two grandfathers but I know they aren't like my grandfather. They don't camp and one lives in Greece. My grandpa and I used to camp a lot on weekends, and in the holidays. Our first serious bushwalk was when I was ten — camping out more than one night, carrying all our gear. Mum had fussed, wanting to pack everything. Grandpa had to repack because he said we wouldn't make it carrying the whole house on our shoulders, and Mum had laughed and given up. Backpacks in the car, we finally headed off for the fire trail. Tingles ripple down my spine when I think about the fire trail. It had been three days of heavy trekking.

* * *

A black snake slid through the bush right across our path, but Grandpa had a stick. Black snakes can kill you but I wasn't scared. We had to be careful of the kookaburras, because they would dive down for our food. I wasn't scared of them either, even though their beaks sometimes drew blood. They aren't cute like Willie wagtails or colourful like lorikeets. Some people say kookaburras are ordinary, but those squawky birds don't know they are ordinary and they fly around as if they are kings of the bush.

We sat on a rock in a creek with the water splashing. We had competitions over who could skim pebbles farthest downstream. You had to choose the right pebble, a smooth one that wasn't too heavy or too light. Then there was the special throwing swing with your arm in the right position. Throwing the rock was real technique. Grandpa had a special spin. I beat Grandpa a few times. I know now that he let me.

I liked throwing pebbles, the blue-tongue lizards, camping under the stars, but the trekking made my feet hurt and the skin was rubbed raw between my legs. I didn't want to walk any more and I stopped. 'I'm tired, Grandpa.'

Grandpa stopped.

'Can we go home?'

Grandpa took my backpack onto his shoulders. 'Home? You are home, Sam.'

I looked at Grandpa because it wasn't true.

'Sam, you're with me.'

I didn't know what he meant, then.

We sang songs and Grandpa told me funny stories. The fire trail went faster and my feet didn't hurt as much and I walked with my legs a bit apart so that they didn't rub.

That night, Grandpa put cream on my feet and the inside of my legs. We drank tea with powdered milk and lots of sugar and ate spaghetti from a can. 'Sam, I'm proud of you. This is a long, hard trek for a boy.'

I felt like a man.

I look at Jones. He has his arm stretched out, looking at the compass. I turn back to see the group following. We're moving forward but it is hard and the skin between my legs rubs together. I walk with my feet a bit apart so that it isn't so sore. The sun has moved from belting down on us to slowly descend towards the west. It's getting cooler. I take a drink. I saw Laura last weekend. She is really beautiful with long brown hair that curls when she walks. She has the sexiest smile and bum. We talk on the phone every day. I don't know what we talk about, but it's great. I love her. Mum says she is GI — Geographically Impossible. She lives on the other side of the harbour. I see her on Saturdays. Saturdays are worked out perfectly. I leave home straight after getting showered and changed from soccer. I check the bus timetable. Then, three minutes walk to the bus stop. Thirty-three minutes by bus to the harbour, race to the ferry. Forty-one minutes on the ferry. Ten minutes walk, then I'm at the front door. Easy.

The guys are always talking about this girl, that girl, their tits — little ones, big ones — showing off how far they have gone. Laura is out of bounds. Talk about her and I'll beat them to a pulp. Andrew and Robbo nearly beat each other to a pulp a couple of weeks ago about a girl. Well, it wasn't really about the girl.

* * *

Everyone met at the usual place, the harbour beach in the National Park. It is a good place to meet. Even Watts hangs out there. No police, no parents, no one telling you to move on. Usually a few yachts are moored in the cove and sometimes night-time scuba divers practise in the water near the cliffs. It is a protected beach and small waves thump onto the sand. There is a weak light from one lamppost. Mostly we hang around on the beach. There were a few cans of beer, vodka mixes, soft drinks and smokes. I drank a record seven cans of cola. Luke took a football since he's football obsessed. In summer there is some skinny-dipping. Not me. I like to keep my pants on, unless there is a good reason. Guys laughing at the size, shape, colour, or whatever, of my dick, isn't great.

There were the usual ones who went off making out in the bushes. Some didn't bother about the bushes and just made out on the sand. Robbo was on the sand deep-throat kissing with a girl.

The next day at school Andrew couldn't help himself. He had to have a go at Robbo in the Physics Lab. 'How'd it taste? Did you like to suck off her tongue?'

'You wouldn't know, would you? No one would want to kiss your ugly face. What's it to you, anyway?'

'Watts? That's right. Watts rings a bell.' Andrew winked at me. 'That girl you were kissing. She'd just been down on Watts. Hmmm. Did you like the taste of him?'

Robbo went this sick egg yolk colour. Guys were starting to throw in a few comments. There were sneers and jokes. That was all Andrew needed — 'You'd kiss anyone.' 'Spunky chick.' 'Licking Watts's arse.'

Robbo started to shove. Andrew shoved back. 'Rumble' buzzed between the test tubes and green lab benches. Guys sat on benches or stood on chairs, giving Andrew and Robbo plenty of room to destroy each other.

Andrew threw a few weak punches at Robbo's head. One accidentally grazed the top of his lip. Andrew looked around grinning. I shook my head but the others were stirring him on. 'Good one, Andrew.' 'Give it to him.' 'Let's see a real fight.'

Robbo licked the top of his lip. Stiffening his body, he flexed his arms into hammers. Andrew wasn't looking. Too obsessed with smart-arse comments.

'Watch it,' I called out to Andrew.

Clenching his hands, Robbo swung his fist with full force into Andrew's stomach. A surprised look rippled down Andrew's face before he reeled back. He was confused. Robbo was raging. He swung, left, right, right, left, hitting stomach, chest, arm, head. Andrew couldn't get his balance and was rocking like a punching bag. Couldn't defend himself against the punches and the blood lust of cheering yahoos. Andrew fell against the tap on the bench, ripping his shirt, the tap jabbing into the small of his back. He was outclassed and . . . punch, fall, breaking glass. I started to move in. Had to do something.

A voice, 'Stop it, you idiots.' Seaten was holding up his hands. Robbo was psycho and kept going until Seaten grabbed his shoulder and Robbo stopped. Andrew wasn't looking great, but he sure looked relieved. Andrew's left eye was already swelling. Five test tubes, two glass beakers and two Bunsen burners were smashed.

Robbo and Andrew spent the afternoon cleaning up and Seaten said that they were 'in debt for the cost of repair and replacement'. Seaten interrogated them, but didn't call their parents. 'Too disgusting,' he said.

The guys are jealous of me. It is Laura. They won't admit it, but what they want is a girlfriend. One-night stands are okay but they usually happen at a drunken party. You hardly remember it and afterwards you have to start hunting again. A girlfriend is different. She's someone you can talk to, muck about with, kiss, go further, lots further. Naked is good. Internet porno sites, magazines and dirty jokes are a bit boring when compared to the real thing. A girlfriend. Some guys hang around me because they think it will rub off. Like getting a girlfriend is contagious. Maybe if they didn't use lines like, 'I like you. Do you want to screw?', or 'I think of you when I wank,' or 'Has anyone told you that you have great tits?' they might have a chance. If Jones wanted, he could get away with it, because he's captain of the First Fifteen, but not normal guys. They are fishing with the wrong bait. You have got to have the nerve to talk to a girl about things that are real and see if she will keep talking to you. There is hope after that.

I have been practising on Mum for years. When I want something, like a lift to school or some money to take Laura to the cinema, I tell her about school and sports, but the masterpiece is the compliment. 'Your hair looks really pretty today, Mum.' Mum knows it is a con job, but she still laughs and I usually get the lift and some money.

There is no Mum to con here. There's no Laura, but there are plenty of idiots. I look back and see Robbo walking behind with Watts. He is wearing the same army boots, gear and marine-style haircut as Watts. Robbo isn't very bright. Bottom grade in all his subjects. Watts is in the bottom grade, too, but he is there for other reasons. He's such a loser. Someone should get him.

'How's it going?' I ask Jones.

He doesn't slow his pace. 'Just got to get to the top of this ridge. It's flat after that. Then it won't matter so much if it's dark.' I would like it better if Jones would talk about stuff, just anything. I know Andrew is insane, but at least he laughs, mucks around, says something about his life. Jones is a good guy, but he's focussed on football or setting up the tent or studying. He's an A-grade student. There has to be something else. Well, maybe not. Maybe that's him, a frozen Viking.

The muscles at the back of my legs throb and I am tired. I take a gulp of iodine water. Tastes like metal but I'm getting used to it. I can hear Spano whining that he can't walk any more. It's a lie.

George and his dixie are okay. The sun is finally setting as we reach the ridge top. I stop to take a breath, look around, rub the back of my legs.

Jones powers on. The others follow. Bennie nods at me as he kicks past. It's funny about his name. His surname sounds like a first name. I don't even know his first name. Maybe he's Bennie Bennie. I nod back at him, then shift aside, moving towards the cliff edge. The rock face is broken into jagged outcrops. Trees cling on here and there to ledges of soil, desperately holding onto the ridge. I carefully look over the cliff. There are a series of cliffs plunging like knives into valleys of gums. My stomach cramps. I watch the shades of green in the valleys change with the last rays of light. The tramping, voices, human sounds are becoming faint as the troop head towards the night campsite. I'm not going with them. Squatting, I watch and wait. I don't know what I'm waiting for. There are only bush sounds, scents of eucalyptus, grey-pink galahs flying home. Home. Suddenly I gasp like a surge of pain. Home. I never thought Grandpa would leave me.

Sarah's voice startles me. 'Beautiful, isn't it?'

I don't answer her.

She crouches beside me.

I glance at her for a second, then turn away. The valley is changing with the light fading and the temperature dropping.

'We'd better move on.'

Why is she talking to me? Why is she here? I keep looking into the valleys. I want to stay here. I don't want to walk alongside Jones who can't talk, or Watts who would stub cigarettes into my arm if he could, or Seaten with his bloody cave. I don't want to carry the dixie on my back. I want to be ten, trekking with my grandpa on the fire trail.

'It's getting dark, Sam.'

'Yes, it's getting dark.'

We wait until there isn't any more light. 'Sam,' she speaks quietly. 'Are you ready?'

No. 'Yes.'

CHAPTER 7

A catheter slides from under his sheets dropping into a bag of urine. Grandpa couldn't piss by himself any more. He couldn't talk. Grandpa was never afraid, but I knew he was afraid here. I pressed my forehead against his bed. I wanted to do something, something.

I wanted him to die . . .

'What? What?' Someone is shoving me. A wave of nausea pounds through my stomach. I'm not sure where I am. Push, shove, push. George is pulling at my sleeping bag, forcing me to wake up. George has the torch light in my face. I squint at him. 'Turn that bloody thing off.' Jones is already awake. Spano is awake and grovelling inside his sleeping bag.

George is pointing. Shadows loom over the tent like mutating beasts. 'Shit,' Jones whispers under his breath. The shadows keep moving, transforming into teeth and claws and huge shapes. Dingoes? Wild pigs? I stretch for my knife. Jones gets his too.

Spano starts to say something but George puts his hand over Spano's mouth. 'Shut up,' George growls in his ear.

I hear the clank of something being pushed. The dixie. I shove my elbow into George. 'Is there food in it?'

He nods.

I hiss. 'Bloody idiot. They're after food.'

A whipping sound hits the tent, thudding like stones. It's going to rip the tent. Spano pisses himself. Jones is out of his sleeping bag, hunched ready to attack. I'm beside him. George is struggling out of his, but I grab his arm. 'Stay.' More whipping sounds. There is pounding. Jones's face is stone and his eyes are piercing. The lump in my throat is rock hard, and my body a coiled spring. I am beside Jones, ready to attack if they break through.

Suddenly there is another sound whipping around our tent. There are running feet. A man's voice cuts the air. 'Get out of there.' Through the gaps, I see Seaten. He is flicking the air with a climbing rope. Sarah is beside him with another rope. There is crashing, thumping, banging of muscular tails as the kangaroos smash down the side of our tent and race away.

Then it is quiet. Jones and I look at each other. I raise my eyebrows. Jones makes a muffled sound. Maybe a laugh.

Sarah bends down alongside us. Seaten stands over her as if on guard. 'Are you all right, Peter? Sam?'

Jones nods at Sarah.

George has still got his hand over Spano's mouth. 'You can let him go, George.' George releases Spano, who is too dazed to irritate us for now.

The kangaroos are gone and we are the butt of everyone's jokes. We're great comic relief after a stinking night sleeping on rocks. Guys are laughing as they pull down their tents and clear the site. 'Kangaroos scared you, did they?' 'Hop over here.' 'Jump. Go on, jump.'

Breakfast is a major comedy routine. The cooking team shout out together, 'Come and get it. Kangaroo stew for breakfast.'

'Better than the usual crap,' I shout back.

Then it's all on. Jumping jokes, boxing kangaroo jokes, porridge awards for bravery. George says nothing, as he was the one who lured the kangaroos to our site. As the guardian of the dixie, the dixie is George's responsibility, especially at night. During the day, most of the guys have been taking turns at carrying the dixie. There was a bit of grumbling at first, but everyone knew it was unfair for one person to carry that great heavy pot on his back for the whole camp. But at night, the dixie belongs to George.

Seaten is shovelling 'kangaroo stew' into his mouth, when he calls out, 'Your *bash* last night really *jumped*.' He laughs. It isn't that funny.

There are so many jokes that Jones and George and I end up laughing. It is pretty hilarious being stampeded by kangaroos desperate for George's dinner leftovers. It's pretty funny the way Jones and I moved straight into crack commando team mode with knives and rearguard action, working out brilliant strategies against the enemy. That ferocious enemy was tough and fast and fluffy. We had to laugh.

Spano isn't laughing. Spano has really got up everyone's noses. Lugging Spano's gear around for him because of his 'sore' ankle has gone down like rotting meat. Since the Sumo win against Robbo, George isn't a major target. He's a good guy. That doesn't mean he isn't punched or the butt of a joke — everyone is at one time or another. But Spano is the real target and pissing his pants has set him up. As we pack gear, Watts really gets into him. He has been edgier than ever. Watts sneers at Spano, calling him 'Piss-head', 'Spisso', 'Piss-pan'. Robbo and other guys join in. Spano tells them to 'shut up', 'get lost', then 'piss off'. That makes everyone roll around laughing.

Everyone is good-humoured trekking to the base of the mountain, with jokes about the kangaroo attack and Spano. We actually forget how tired we are. Even Bennie smiles at Luke's re-enactment of the kangaroo invasion. Bennie doesn't usually smile much. We arrive at the mountain's base in not too bad a mood. Then we see it. The mountain. I have to bend my head as far back as I can to sight the top. It has to be a forty-five degree climb. There is a sheer rise to the peak. Staring down at us, the mountain hovers like a giant gremlin.

It hadn't looked so steep when I saw it on the map. Jones isn't worried. He enjoys a challenge; he'd enjoy climbing the Himalayas with a broken leg. Luke looks okay about it, too, which is what you'd expect from an extreme sports fanatic. Sarah goes to check how steep is the rise a bit further down the track. Seaten follows her. I reckon he has a thing for Sarah. It's insane. As if she's interested. The rest of us normal human beings aren't so happy. Well, that is the wrong word for it. Aggressive, agitated, pissed off. 'Bloody not doing it.' 'What's this shit?' 'Who's the idiot who planned this?'

'Stop being lazy bums,' I throw back at them. I pretend to be tough. 'Can't you climb a bloody little hill like that?'

'You're got a bloody little brain. That's the problem, Knox.' Watts lets out a sarcastic grunt. He grinds his knuckle into my arm. He's coming down from something for sure.

I'm not in a mental state for Watts. I just hate the dickhead. 'Touch me, and I'll break your face.'

Watts raises his fist to hit me, but Jones grabs his arm. 'We're going up the mountain.' His voice is hard. Watts stares at him. Jones stares back. Robbo stands behind Watts. I stand behind Jones. I'm ready for a punch-up. Get it over and done with or start a war. I don't care any more. Watts is a jackass. No, I mean jack-arse. Adrenaline is pumping. There's going to be blood.

Crash. I jump back. The dixie bangs on the ground like a hammer smashing metal. It's George. Fat George with his round, red face and the smell of pasta. He bellows out a joke, throwing the dumbest gag into the ring. 'Boxing kangaroos.' He pretends to box and I notice nervous sweat trickle down his neck. 'Looks like we'll have a bit of fun with kangaroos if we stay at the bottom of the mountain. We can make great jumpers.'

We stare at George, speechless. He's still boxing the air. Watts is the first to recover. 'I'll stuff a jumper down your throat. You're shit scared of kangaroos,' Watts sneers.

'That's me. Scared of kangaroos, and rabbits too.'

'What are you talking about, George?' Luke calls out.

'You're a freak, George.' Watts's hands are in his army pants pockets now.

'That's me. Freaky George and the kangaroos.' There's a slight stutter, more sweat, then bravado. 'We'd better hop along.'

'Shut up, George.' Robbo looks at Watts.

Watts and Jones glare at each other. Watts shakes his head. 'Forget it.' They turn away.

George is standing there flushed and sweating. I didn't know he had it in him. George, who sat up like a right angle afraid to sleep. George who is terrified that Watts will kill him. George who I promised to protect. He's wiping the sweat from the back of his neck. George was afraid. It's tough to make a stand when you're afraid. I grab George's arm and twist it around to his back. He spins around and I say in his ear, 'Thanks, George.' Before I let go, I whisper, 'mate'.

Jokes and the mountain. Backpack straps are pulled hard, securing the contents, shoelaces are tightened, insect repellent and sunscreen rubbed into faces. Then it is serious climbing. Jones volunteers to take the dixie. It's strapped on top of his backpack. The rocks provide uneven ledges to grab onto. We scrape between the trees, tearing off slabs of bark as we hold onto the ghost gums. Saplings are nearly torn out of the ground as they are grabbed in desperate attempts not to tip backwards. 'Snake' echoes down the line. I look at the ground, but our boots go right up to our ankles. Even if you confront a snake, its fangs will dig into rubber and leather, not flesh.

The temperature is rising as the morning sun starts to beat down and the flies get ready for mass attacks. In some parts, we have to crawl on our hands and knees up the tracks. Gravel scrapes tear my hands. I suck my hand to get the sting out. I don't understand why we're doing this. Maybe they want us to hate the bush? I hold onto a tree, pulling myself forward. Got to keep going. Watts lands on his stomach, scrambles back onto his knees, kicking the rocks so hard that bits break off. He's going to smash someone's head in. 'Hey, control it, Watts,' Seaten barks. Everyone keeps out of Watts's way. He'd be nearly out of cigarettes by now, even with rationing his smokes at night. He hides with his mates behind his bivvy, lighting up. Stale nicotine hangs around Watts like dying smog. You'd think Seaten would notice.

The peak is hours away. I squint, staring upwards to the mountain top. An eagle is flying over the gum trees, soaring like the world belongs to it. I've only seen an eagle in the wild twice. I slow down to watch it. Why wasn't I born an eagle? It dives into another valley and it is gone. I look ahead and can just see Jones scrambling over a fallen tree trunk. In the movies everyone starts singing at this point, trudging courageously but happily into the unknown. Bloody fools.

There's a yell. I look around. George is sliding backwards. The gravelly stones are acting like grease. 'Shit.' He's getting up speed. George has flattened Spano. 'Hold onto the trees, you idiot,' I scream out, trying to move back towards him.

George's mouth opens like an owl. A howling moan reverberates through the bush as he hits dirt. Seaten is suddenly there. He grabs onto a tree with one hand and grabs George with the other, actually stopping his momentum. George stops sliding. Seaten's muscles bulge and I gain a limited respect for him.

'Hold on, Sumo,' echoes down the track.

'Holding,' George eventually grunts, catching his breath.

Sarah calls down. 'Are you okay?'

George puffs. 'Just slipped. Lost my grip.'

'You got to watch those gravelly rocks. Slippery stuff.' Seaten waits until George is ready to start climbing again. George is ready.

'It's okay.' Seaten signals the troop to start moving again.

I wait for George to climb up to me.

Midday. The sun is a fireball. There is no stopping for lunch today. Everyone is careful about their water and they take calculated sips. We keep moving. Guys strip down to their T-shirts. Flies land in battalions on Robbo. He's carrying the plastic garbage and burnt cans. It's a magnet for every fly in the bush. Saves the rest of us from mass attack. The flies land on Robbo's back and arms and he can hardly see. He keeps swiping them away with this black-infested arm. They are up his nose, in his ears, devouring sweat from his face. He can't speak without the risk of being choked by a internal fly invasion. I actually feel sorry for Robbo. The flies must be three centimetres deep on his back. George and I follow him having bets. 'Whoever grabs the most wins.' I take a swipe and get a fistful. I let them go one at a time through a one-fly opening I make between my hands. 'One, two, three, four . . . eleven.' I shove George. 'Beat that.'

George has a turn. Twelve. I have a turn. Ten. Then the competition becomes fierce. Fourteen. Seventeen. Fifteen . . . Then George does it. He takes one huge grab that nearly knocks Robbo over, except Robbo doesn't mind. He's pretty glad we're getting flies off him.

'Nineteen,' I admire. 'You're definitely the champion, George.'

It is even steeper now and everyone is on their hands and knees, dragging themselves forwards. No one is talking. There is concentration on the ground, trying to ignore the pain in legs and arms. I leave George and move up the line to get away from Robbo's flies. He can't even brush them away now. Sarah is in front of me and I try to keep pace with her. My legs are lead. I watch the muscles of her calves tighten, contracting as she climbs. I don't even have one sexy joke about her. There's just pain. The pain in my legs is nearly unbearable and there's another hour before we hit the landing. Just keep moving. Just keep moving. Sarah's boots are magnets as I follow her climb. She turns for a second to look back and check, then smiles at me. Her smile is like Laura's. It's hard to lift my arms. Laura. Spasms. Focus on Laura. Her smile. That first time she smiled at me was at Pizza Palace.

She dropped into the shop to buy pizza that night. She ordered the barbecue chicken pizza and smiled. One of those drop-dead gorgeous smiles. I was gone. Long brown wavy hair, green eyes, a voice like an angel. I asked her for her order again. She laughed. I wanted to talk to her, but it was pretty difficult when all these deadhead customers were waiting to place orders. I ignored them for as long as I could until the boss told me to get my act together. She waited for me to give her the pizza and then she left and I thought I would never see her again.

Laura bought a lot of pizza. Every Saturday night for a month. Then she gave me her phone number for a takeaway order, but she picked up the pizza herself anyway. I wrote the number down in the order book and put it on the computer, then on a bit of paper and stuffed it in my pocket. All that night I kept thinking about her phone number. It was burning a hole in my pocket. When I got home after work, I stuck it on my wall.

Should I ring her? You can lose your job if you ring a customer for a date, not a pizza. The risk. If I rang, she could say it wasn't like that — she could report me to the boss. She could laugh at me and tell everyone that I made an idiot of myself. Every day for two weeks I kept looking at that phone number, scribbling notes and drawings around it. Will I? Won't I? Yes. No.

I ambled towards the phone. It is a cream, touch dial, ordinary phone. Nothing threatening, except I started sweating as I picked up the receiver. 'It's only a phone, for God's sake,' but I knew I was lying to myself. It was like headbutting a soccer ball. Grit your teeth and go for it. It might dent your head, crack your neck, but it could be a winner. Dial. The tone was loud. Maybe she wasn't at home. Three rings.

'Hello, Laura here.'

Her voice was like a sweet orange.

'Hello, anyone there?'

Pause. 'It's me.' That was so stupid. Who's me? I could be the local newspaperman for all she knew.

'Hi, Sam.'

Sam. She recognised my voice. Sam.

Then it was easy, like talking in the pizza shop. Easy. We rang each other a lot after that. There was the big date at the cinema where I held her hand. Her soft hand with silver rings that I could rotate. She smelt like the sea. There was that afternoon walk to the park. We clasped palms all along the street past shops, houses, barking dogs. She was scared of the pit bull terrier and she held my hand tighter. When she saw the park, she let go and started running. 'Catch me if you can,' she giggled, running with her hair blowing in the wind. She was fast and I laughed. I watched her bum in her blue jeans. She has a great bum. Her tits bounced under her black T-shirt. I started running after her. 'Watch out, Laura.' She ran faster, her hair wisping into knots. I ran faster. I started gaining pace and with a burst of energy I caught up to her, tackling her onto the long grass. I pinned her down under the fig trees, kissing her soft lips, wet with the sweet taste of her, breathing her short breaths until she wasn't puffing any more and she was kissing me back.

We will be having our three-month anniversary when I get back from camp. Mum gave me the condom talk which was a real low point in our mother–son relationship. I think about Laura at night and in the day sometimes. She's five months older than me. Seventeen and three months. Andrew thinks that it's great that she is 'an older woman'. 'She's got to be experienced.' He's such an idiot. I'm her first real boyfriend. She stayed over late one night and she let me suck her tits. It was great, but she doesn't want sex. She has to be in love with me. Well, I'm in love with her. I know I am. Why isn't she in love with me? She will be. I've just got to wait. I respect her a lot. I'm going to buy her something special for our anniversary. I've saved some money already. I don't want to be cheap. Maybe I'll get her a gold bracelet with our initials engraved on it. I've just got to save a bit more.

The line is stopping. I look up and Sarah is standing on a small flat stretch of land. Backpacks are being thrown onto the ground and guys are lying spreadeagled in the dirt. I follow them. There is groaning and grumbling as the last of the guys make it up to the flat section. Jones unstraps the dixie from his back and rests against a boulder. I stretch my arms and legs. Sarah comes over with some heat rub. 'Pass it around.' She hands it to Luke. 'It'll help those sore muscles.'

'I think a shower, shave, television and a chicken burger might help a bit more.'

'Chicken burger for me.'

'Me too.'

'Shower.'

'A stretcher would be great. Who's going to carry me down?'

'No chicken burgers or showers,' Sarah laughs.

Other guys just head off for private spaces and rub the ointment into their muscles. There's no more joking. Too exhausted. I look at my watch. Three o'clock. The sun isn't as hot and the air up here is thinner, cooler. It feels better, but when the sun goes down it'll be different. Freezing cold and we're at the top of a mountain. The flat isn't big enough for us to all camp. We can't stay here.

Seaten calls out. 'Over this way.' No one moves. Seaten is standing next to two sheer rock faces. 'We're going up this.'

'Shit.'

CHAPTER 8

Sarah is standing against the vertical shaft: 'the chimney'. Two rock faces confront each other like the shields of warring Greek gods. I've always liked those stories of Hercules and Zeus. Big-picture wars with superhuman gods fighting for power. We're so high here. Nearly at the peak. I stare at the rising rocks. Twenty-five metres at least. My back prickles. It has a mythological feel, like we are part of legendary heavens and ancient battles. Grandpa used to say Australia is an ancient country. It feels ancient.

Sarah's voice is insistent. 'You're all going to climb this.' She crinkles her eyes, staring at every one of us. 'I know you can do it.' She nods at Bennie. 'Even you.' Bennie looks at his knee that is still bleeding from his fall. Tripped over a ridge, or maybe threw himself over it. Luckily, it was a small one.

Everyone is still sore from the grope up the mountain and we're starving. There are a few laughs — 'Sure', 'Easy'. Luke's bivvy group lets out a joint grunt. It looks like they have bonded. The Principal should be happy. Jones punches the air with a controlled fist,

Robbo rumbles, 'No problem,' but George doesn't say anything. He just drags his pack behind him.

Watts brushes gravel from his army pants, looks at the chimney and then at George. 'As long as I'm not following fat-arse George, it's fine,' Watts spits a blob of saliva into the dirt. 'Wouldn't want to be crushed by that blubbering heap of shit.'

'Shut up, Watts.' Jones gives him a contemptuous look.

Watts laughs, but I can see his sneer. Watts doesn't like Jones.

I walk beside George. 'Are you all right?'

'Sure.' George straightens up.

Jones has done rock climbing before. He's one of those guys who can hang vertical by his fingers from a cliff. Unbelievable stuff. He helps Seaten prepare the gear for the pulley that every climber is roped onto to protect them from a fall.

Sarah instructs the rest of us on how we connect to the rope. Since Luke is the extreme sports fanatic, she makes him demonstrate the way to get into a harness. It's like stepping into a seat made of straps that go around your legs and waist, with other straps that connect them all together. There's a loop at the front to attach the rope. Everyone has worn a harness before for abseiling. So it's pretty uninteresting stuff until Sarah tightens the straps around Luke's waist. It's like a chain reaction below his belt. She's pulled it too hard. Hard is the right word. The straps dig in on both sides of his dick. Luke looks like a porno king. He's jumping around. We're nearly pissing ourselves laughing. Even Sarah is laughing. Luke finally undoes it and flings the harness at us. 'Very funny, you pack of hyenas.' He stomps away.

Seaten calls out. 'What's all the commotion?'

'Nothing,' Sarah calls back to him. 'Okay guys, okay. Let's settle down. It's my fault.' The laughing subsides. Sarah shouts, waving to Luke. 'My fault, Luke. Really sorry.'

He comes back grumbling. 'Right.'

Sarah puts the harness on herself this time to demonstrate. She holds up a karabiner, which is a metal clip with a spring-loaded gate. She puts it through the loop on the front of her harness. 'The karabiner can take twenty-seven kilo-Newtons which means about 2.7 tonnes of weight.'

'Fat George should be fine then.' I elbow him.

'Shut up.' George elbows me back.

'You'll all be alright. It's designed to take a fall which is much more than any of you weigh.' Sarah demonstrates as she talks. 'The ropes from the pulley go through the karabiner. The karabiner is the only thing that connects you directly to your harness and the pulley system. That's why there's an additional lock here.' Sarah makes us all lock on a karabiner to a harness, then runs rope through it until she's satisfied that we're all okay with it.

'You have got two things to do on the chimney. Any ideas?'

'Smoke. Or go up in smoke.' Guys are laughing. 'What about climbing it?' I look up at the chimney. It's steep.

'Yes, you climb it. That's one thing. The other really important thing is to belay.'

'What's that?' Spano squeaks. I give him a filthy stare. Even opening his mouth aggravates me.

'You mean who does the belaying. The belayer is the man-on-the-ground who holds the end of the pulley rope, which is tied to the climber. He'll break your fall if you have one. He's your security.'

'Sounds really great.' 'Good way to knock someone off.' 'Oops, sorry, accidentally let you smash onto the ground.'

'You're all comedians.' Sarah flicks the climbing rope in front of her. 'But it does mean that you have to trust someone with your life.'

That makes me feel terrific.

'If you fall, the belayer pulls the rope and activates the belay plate. It's like a brake. It stops the fall and you'll only drop a metre or so.'

'We'll be hanging around,' Spano calls out.

I didn't know Spano had a brain, let alone one that was capable of making a joke. A pathetic joke. That little shit has still got a 'sore ankle' and can't carry his gear. The rotten part is that the chimney will be easy for him. He's small and quick but he had better watch out who's holding the rope. He might end up falling more than a few metres. On his head, if we're lucky, except we'd have to carry him out. Who could be bothered? He'd probably live as well.

'I hope there isn't too much hanging around,' Sarah smiles.

Let's get on with it. The climb. I'm getting sick of all this talking.

Sarah goes on about the climb itself. 'You slide up one rock face with your back against it and you press your feet against the other face. Then push upwards.' She demonstrates the moves, explains climbing techniques like weight transfer on your feet, edging, gripping techniques. She asks for questions. There are some, then answers. More questions. Answers.

I zip up my jacket. It's getting cold and the air feels harder to breathe. I watch Sarah talk but her words are disappearing into boulders and bush. My stomach rumbles and even sand is looking good. Sarah's thermals are greyer than a few days ago and her tits are looking smaller. It feels great touching Laura's big, soft breasts. Her nipples are pinkish and stand out. I like it when she doesn't wear a bra. Then my great tickle plan is activated. I always play around and tickle her and get plenty of free feels as she tries to get away. Excellent. Andrew made out one night with a girl with flattish nipples. Well, he said they were flat, before he went into every other detail of her body. I guess there are lots of nipple shapes. Con wouldn't know what a real nipple looks like. Poor Con.

I watch Jones run his hand over the rock surface. It gives me the shivers. Rough rock and soft breasts. Jones knows about breasts though. He's had a girlfriend for nearly a year. They're having sex. Lucky bastard. I'm really hanging out for it, except I love Laura. Jones doesn't love his girlfriend. He'd rather go out with the guys unless it's for sex. He keeps her waiting around and she just has to be there when he feels like seeing her or when he wants to make out. She's pretty cute. I don't get why she stays with him, except she doesn't think much of herself. Laura told me that her parents fight a lot. I'd hate that. Maybe having just one parent isn't too bad. She shows off to her girlfriends that she's dating the captain of the First Fifteen. Maybe she screws him for that.

Jones doesn't cheat on her or talk about the sex, even though everyone knows he's having it with her. It's just that she isn't that important to him and he'll dump her when he's ready. He says that she understands that they're only friends. He's still a good guy, but he must know it is more than that for her.

Seaten already has the rope over his shoulder and is ready to monkey up the wall when Jones asks Sarah, 'Can I set up the climb?'

'Muscle man.' 'The Spiderman of the Bush.' There are laughs and cheers.

'Spiderman. Sure.' Jones grins.

'It is challenging,' Sarah says slowly.

'Oh yeah, we know it's the challenge,' Luke yells out.

'Well, some can take it and some can't.' Sarah raises her eyebrows at Jones. 'You have to set up the fall breaks. There is no belayer at the bottom for you.'

'I know. I've done it before.' Jones waits. 'A lot of times.'

Sarah hesitates, kicks a rock, then nods. 'If you can do it, then go for it, Peter.' Sarah squints at him. 'You'd better not kill yourself.'

Seaten isn't so sure, but Jones is. Jones knots the laces of his boots, grabs the climbing rope. He links one end of it into a karabiner lock, then clips it onto his belt. There are already bolts in place from previous climbs, but he takes extra wedges to put into rock cracks for added protection against free falls. Seaten double checks the gear. 'You're right to go?'

Jones squints up at the shaft. The descending sun glares into his eyes. The chimney looks unclimbable. 'Right to go,' he says. Jones stretches out his arms, flexing his muscles so that even his blond hairs seem to expand. Everyone stops complaining about digging shit holes, blistered feet, backpacks chafing shoulder blades and rotten food. Wherever we are — leaning against a boulder or sitting on the ground or mid-sentence — we watch. We watch Jones ascend: Jones hanging by his hands; Jones threading rope through the bolts to break any falls; Jones zigzagging between small edges and crevices that give him footholds and handholds. He hauls himself up higher bit by bit, locking his hands into narrow crevices in the rock or digging his fingers into small holes and cracks. Slowly he crisscrosses the vertical rock surface, moving upwards towards the peak. He really is Hercules.

As he reaches the top, guys shout out to him. Jones waves before looking around for an anchor to tie the rope, then the karabiner to set up the pulley. There's a final wave before he clambers down the rock face with the rope.

The chimney climb starts.

Seaten is going up first. I wait for my turn, but meanwhile, I'm starving. The cooking megalomaniacs are handing out crispbreads and peanut butter. Mean bastards. I grab my share before jamming my backpack against a tree to eat in peace. I'm tired and bloody hungry. I slouch against my pack, smell my peanut butter crispbread, then bite into it. Only a bit of sand in the peanut butter. Who cares? It tastes good. Then it's gone and my stomach is still vacant. I call out to Bennie who is scooping out peanut butter from a jar to everyone. 'What about extra food?'

Heads turn to Bennie who doesn't react. He just keeps doling out peanut butter. There is something wrong with Bennie. He doesn't seem to hear anything any more. 'More food. More food. More.' There's this Oliver Twist feeling, especially when a couple of guys burst into rap, belting out, 'more, more, more', until Luke and Robbo jump them. 'Shut up, shut up.'

But we're starving and the chimney is going to take hours. Even if everyone is Spano-fast, which is not the case, it'll be a long time before we eat again. I dig out my gloves from my pack. The temperature is starting to seriously drop. It could snow tonight. We'd better not be here on the mountain.

The rumble is over. We're all still hungry. Then a historic moment — consensus. Starvation unites us, even Watts. Food. Food. Food. 'But it's for dinner.' Bennie attempts to stop the attack. He's pushed aside, overrun as hands pull apart the stash. Canned tuna and more canned tuna. We stuff our faces until we lie, stinking of fish and oil, like bloated whales on a mountaintop.

The orgy of tuna eating over, we settle into the afternoon to watch the climbers. Brainless comments entertain everyone for a while — 'Got glue on your feet?' 'Your mother should see you now.' 'Need a bomb up your butt to move.' A tune follows that one with a few disgusting choruses about butts.

Seaten is checking the belay gear, giving orders. Sarah is checking the harnesses and karabiners. Some guys are okay scaling the chimney with only a few falls, but not George. I go over to see what's happening.

He's stuck. Stuck like a lump of cement between one rock face and the other. Even Luke, who is holding the rope, is weakening under the weight. Smart-arse comments avalanche onto Fat George, but he's not listening. His face is red and he's stuck. Sarah climbs up to talk to him, to unlock his fingers jammed into a ledge. 'Let go, George. Let go.' Sarah pleads. He won't. I yell out to him 'Move George, move.' No way. George is stuck and staying that way. I don't know how she does it, but Sarah eventually gets him unstuck. It's crazy.

Suddenly George is swinging like a bloated pendulum between the rock faces, nearly pulling the belayer off his feet. We're yelling to George. He looks down at us, trying to focus, then grits his teeth, 'Okay, okay, I'm going to make this.'

With sweat saturating George's shirt, he plants his feet against one rock face and his back against the other. He shoves himself upwards. Finally he crawls over the ledge out of the chimney. He waves from the top, then raises his fist in victory.

There are two camps now — the top of the chimney and the bottom of the chimney. Guys settle into both. Some nod off, others look at the climbers. Jones and I head for a quiet spot away from the action to talk about post-chimney strategy. 'We can't stay on the mountain tonight, Jones.'

'Too cold and no camping sites.'

'It's a shorter run down the other side of the mountain.'

'I saw a bush cabin on the map. We could camp there, even if it's late.'

'Wouldn't have to set up the tents.'

'We'll have to persuade the rest of them. But after the chimney …' I shove my pack around trying to make it into a pillow.

Jones takes the shit hole spade and heads for private territory. He passes Watts who is edgy. Tinderbox edgy. He's punched Robbo too hard and Robbo's gone off to hug a tree somewhere.

'Why don't you give Robbo a break, Watts?'

'Why don't you bugger off, Jones?'

'You bugger off.' Jones swipes at him, then turns his back.

Jones isn't prepared when Watts goes for him. The punch is fist deep into his kidneys. Jones reels. I race towards him, grabbing Jones, protecting him like a fortress. Watts just stands there. Jones can't get his breath. 'Breathe, Peter, breathe.'

He holds onto his stomach. 'Okay, okay,' Jones gasps. His face is mask rigid. His blue eyes frost into ice. I glare at Watts. Jones will remember this. Watts walks away.

I shout at him, 'You're a fucking lunatic, Watts.'

Something happened at the Rave.

'What's the event?' Guys were crowding into the Men's toilets and some were spilling out. The urinal is usually a slash and run business. 'What's going on?'

Andrew was trying to push his way through from the end of the spill, but he wasn't getting too far.

'I'm trying out the back. Coming?'

'No way,' Andrew shouted at me.

It gets on my nerves, the way Andrew always thinks he knows everything. 'You're a sheep,' I called out.

'Baa,' he bounced back.

That's one thing I like about Andrew, his humour, but I was not joining the flock. I remembered seeing a couple of high windows when I hung a leak at the urinal. I made my way outside into the laneway. It was dark except for the light coming out of the toilet windows. I threaded my way through stinking garbage, broken bottles, decomposing boxes. An old wooden ladder was lying against the wall. That was luck, except when I stood it against the wall most of the rungs were hanging off. Better than nothing.

Getting up was all right, but the windows . . . frosted. Couldn't see a thing. The frames were rotting. There was a jagged chunk of wood missing from one. I reached for it, pulled at it and forced the window open. Just a tug. Another one. Ouch, that bloody hurt. Green paint and rotting wood stuck into my thumb. It was a big piece. Out. Blood. I could get hepatitis. It had better be worth it. Right, I was up. Andrew was going to be angry that I was right. What was happening? Guys, guys everywhere. Robbo, Watts. They meant trouble. No, no, there were a few good mates inside. What were they looking at? Needed to get a bit higher. The next rung looked barely okay. It was creaking and the ladder moved slightly. That was it. If I didn't see anything then I was out of there.

Great, I could see. Okay, what was that? There was a space. Guys watching something. Beer cans on the floor. No one was at the urinals. I started laughing. Some of them are so drunk, they had their pants down and were mooning their bums. Idiots. Robbo was wanking off. He'd lost his brains. They were bloody watching each other wank. This was blackmail stuff. There was Watts. God, he looked manic. His hair was sweaty, dripping wet. He was shoving and pushing. He was on speed big-time. Was someone crying? It sounded like a cat. No, no cat. Watts. I couldn't believe it. Watts is hung like a bull. Just his luck.

What was that? Whimpering. It was really hard to hear. Maybe nothing. I stretched up just a bit higher. Creak. This ladder was going to crash. Landing in the stinking lane on my head was not a great idea. Better get down. What was that? It was something. What? A cat? Hard to see. Guys in the way. This ladder was moving. I thought I saw something. Stuck between beer cans. I saw something.

That bastard Watts.

CHAPTER 9

Slide. The skin of my arms scrapes against the rock face. 'Keep going. You can do it,' Sarah calls out. I grit my teeth and push up. A bit higher, a bit more, I shove my back along the sandstone. I try not to think of the burning in my arms and the rip in my stomach. I press upwards, grunting cloudy donuts into the cold air. It is cold but I'm sweating. Dribbles bounce off my eyebrows like water. I brush them off. Try to balance. 'Shit,' and I drop, hanging like a side of beef. A one-metre fall. The belayer shouts out, 'Right?' There are a few sarcastic comments about my climbing skills. More bonding.

'Right.' I rest for a minute, rubbing my stinging hands. The skin is shredded. There'll be blisters there tonight. I clench my fists, pressing raw fingers into the palms. Squinting, I look at the peak. I'm bloody well getting up this. I clench my jaw and climb, shuffling upwards, grabbing ledges, gripping rock pockets, grazing skin. Come on, Sam. My face is iron. Pull up. Nearly there. Grunting. Nearly. I'm going to do this. The peak. Superhuman effort. Come on, Sam. Nearly. The peak. Over it.

Seaten signals. 'Not bad, Knox.' Then he's focussed again. 'Next,' echoes down the chimney shaft.

I stand looking down the shaft. I shake my hands, letting the cold air freeze the stinging before turning away. I wander between guys lying on the ground getting a bit of rest. A few are grouped together, not talking much. Iodine is being tossed around for hands. Luke throws me the bottle. Spano doesn't need any. It was easy climbing for Spano. Bastard. I stop to look at my hands. The iodine stings as I stain them yellow. I stare at the chimney. No one hauled me up, no rescue attempts. I did it myself. Grandpa would have liked that. He would have done that climb with me. He could do anything. Grandpa. I never missed not having a father.

When I was little I didn't care about not having a father. I didn't think you needed one. What was important were mothers. All sorts. Fat and thin, noisy and quiet, intelligent and bossy. Mothers collected kids from school and worked in the canteen and took you to the doctor's. They shopped in the supermarket where you threw tantrums if you didn't get that toy. Mothers went to playgroups and brought out paints and playdough and sang 'The Wheels of the Bus Go Round and Round'. They took you to pre-school when they worked and collected you afterwards and made dinner. Sometimes when they were tired you'd get take-away which was great. You always hoped they were too tired to make dinner. Sometimes there were fathers at the Saturday morning sports matches, but then I had Grandpa. Grandpa came to parent-teacher nights and took me camping and replaced dripping taps.

Later, from pictures in books, I found out that fathers ate meals with you and brought home money and that they slept in the mother's bed. Before I got too old, I'd sleep in Mum's bed when I had nightmares. Sometimes I'd wet the bed, sometimes I'd kick her all night. Once Mum had a man who slept in her bed, but he never let me lie beside her even when I was scared. He wasn't a father. He didn't stay for breakfast.

I liked breakfasts when I was little. I'd sit with Grandpa and eat Grandpa egg. That was a special soft-boiled egg that you put soldiers into. Not real soldiers. It was bread cut into strips that you dunked into the yellow yolk. I loved the helmet that Grandpa sliced off the top of the egg and put on the side of his eggcup next to a pile of salt. He always scooped out the helmet and gave it to me. 'The best part,' he'd say. It always tasted like the best part. You know, I never said to Grandpa, 'You have it, you have the best part.' I wish I'd done that. Just once.

'Hey, Knox.' Luke throws me a couple of bandages.

'Thanks.' I catch the packet and head to the other side of the peak. I unwrap the bandages and stuff the packing in my pocket for the garbage group. I've been lucky not to get that detail. Maggots crawling up my back — disgusting. Chills crawl along my arms at the thought of it.

The sun is starting to go down. There are no flies here. Too cold and it's getting late. I clamber onto a boulder on the edge of the peak and stare out into valleys and mountains. Ancient mountains. I can hardly breathe. It's so immense. I peer down cliff drops. Is the world at my feet? Sometimes, I feel that I can do anything. I can't wait to leave school. One more year. I'm going to buy a car. Grandpa left me some money. Andrew, Con and I are planning a five-day trek into the Blue Mountains. Afterwards, we're heading north, hitting the beaches, pubs and girls. Except I've got Laura. I hope we'll be having sex by then. How good will it be, when I make love to Laura? I miss her a lot.

Suddenly, I jerk forward. Seaten's shouting cuts through my thoughts, fracturing them. 'Get your gear ready.' I turn around. Everyone has reached the peak now. Jones did the last climb, removed the pins from the rockface. He is rolling up the climbing ropes. Sarah is tying the dixie onto George's back. Robbo's clearing the site of garbage. Spano has his backpack on. Looks like his 'sore ankle' is better since Sarah saw him climb the chimney.

A shadow makes me look up curiously. A hawk glides in the air currents before disappearing between mountains. Wish I was a hawk or an eagle. They don't have to climb the chimney to see the world. I look down at everyone from my boulder. It's a strange feeling. We're like ants on a tiny mountaintop, with all those monumental gullies and landscapes behind. How long would it have taken rivers to cut away those mountains? Millions and millions of years. There is life here and it's not us. Eagles, wallabies, echidnas, possums, spiders … and bush. Amazing bush. Aborigines wandered through this landscape. But this is more than them, more than human beings. It just is. I don't get why we matter, why I matter. Why I feel important sometimes and at other times, like nothing. I don't understand why we feel so much and do what we do. Grandpa said we're part of it and that's why. God's plan. I try not to think of the big picture because I get lost. I try to understand the little picture so that I can find my way.

* * *

I found out I had no father when kids at school pinned me against the toilet wall and called me 'bastard' and called my mother 'slut'. They belted the shit out of me. Mum put iodine on my cut lip and hugged me for a long time and said she loved me. Grandpa taught me to fight.

Mum spoke in her quiet way and said Grandpa was better than any father. I knew that was true.

Mum made me go to Sunday School because I had no father. She felt guilty about it. She wanted me to know about God. Grandpa used to walk to the church with me, but he'd never go inside. He'd touch his chest: 'God is in here.' There were other kids there and I got to colour pictures of Jesus and Christmas trees. I liked the Christmas story about Mary having Jesus in a stable. God did it. Jesus was the son of God. I thought about that for ages and eventually worked out that that was how I was born. God was my father. Immaculate conception. After I worked that out, I wouldn't miss even one Sunday School. The teacher thought I was amazing because I kept asking all these questions about how Jesus was born and the angels and the stable.

But one day I found the photo of Mum holding me as a baby in the hospital. She looked sad, not like Mary in Sunday School pictures. I forced Mum to tell me. She cried and said she was so happy I was born but . . . God wasn't my father. He was a seventeen-year-old boy in Mum's class. He had a name. Paul. She was in love and he didn't use a condom. It was her final year at school and she finished her exams and had a baby. He finished his exams and never saw her again. He never saw me. I didn't go to Sunday School after that.

Jones calls me to come over. Decision time. There is still some light and we can't camp here. Temperatures are starting to seriously dive. Scrogan is being passed around. Scrogan is good. It's a huge bag of chaff — small, crummy bits of muesli, deformed nuts, moth-eaten dried fruits, biscuit shreds, chocolate bit rejects. Guys kill for the chocolate bits.

'Hey, Sumo, get your bloody hand out of it.'

George laughs. 'Don't worry, I've left a couple of sucked-out raisins.'

Scrogan means moving on. No dinner now. We ate all the tuna anyway. The plan is to abseil down the other side of the chimney, and even if it is dark head down the mountain. Everyone agrees. No one wants to be lying on rocks in the freezing cold on top of this mountain without enough air to breathe. It could snow. Jones excites everyone when he mentions the bush cabin. He points to the map. 'The bush cabin is here. Not far from the river.'

Yeah. No bivvys tonight. A cabin will save us an hour making camp and it'll be luxury. A floor, instead of dirt. No doors, no kitchen, no bathroom, broken windows, but there'll be a roof. Probably leaking, but then it doesn't look like rain. Estimated time of arrival. Midnight.

'Let's abseil.' 'Great.' Exhaustion changes to energy. Everyone has done it before. Harnesses on. Clicked in. Rope secured around an anchor; not Sumo George but my boulder. We're off. Luke is a wild man. He lets out this blood-curdling scream and does a mighty leap backwards, hurtling down the cliff. I follow. There is just one moment of fear before I leap backwards when I look down that cliff face. A stab of panic. It's a long, long jump. Then the plunge. Blood rush. I'm flying. Pounding off the cliff face. Jerking back again into the air. Flying. Fantastic.

Abseiling the cliff is fast. Even George makes it okay. Seaten is last. Everyone is cheering him as he runs down the cliff forwards. He flips back just before he hits dirt at the bottom. Sarah shouts at him, 'Dangerous example,' but he's adrenaline flooded and higher than on speed.

We're off the peak. Harnesses are packed away. Torches out and on. Backpacks checked. Jones and I have another look at the map, working out the quickest and safest way to the cabin. We check the direction against the compass.

'Don't lose sight of the person in front,' Sarah lectures everyone. 'Call out to wait, if that happens. Right?' No one answers. 'Right?'

'Sure. Yeah. Okay.'

'Let's move it,' Jones calls out.

The light from the moon is much brighter than in the city. No city lights. We start our downward climb trailing in line one after the other. Our torches flash on rocky soil and the backpack in front, while the moon acts like a bleary headlight. It's going to be a long night.

There is talking for about an hour, intermittent insults for the next hour, then silent trudging. No one is interested any more in how great the abseiling was or how George got stuck up the chimney or how they hate Spano. It's freezing and legs are hurting. It should have been easier going downhill, but it isn't. Our knees grate with every downward step and calf muscles tighten into steel dumbbells. It's walking with the brakes on. Guys get into lower gear sliding down gravelly parts, navigating slowly between trees. It doesn't help the pain. It might as well be fourth gear, except fourth gear would probably mean crashing into each other as well.

'Where's the bloody cabin, Jones?'

'Where's the bloody cabin, Jones?'

'Where's the bloody cabin, Jones?'

The question echoes down the line

'Not far,' he shouts back, but Jones shows me the map and I know he's not sure where the cabin is. I'm glad he's the leader and not me.

One in the morning and there is still no cabin, but there is still plenty of downhill trekking. Spano trips, sliding into Watts who shoves him into a tree. Lucky that's all it is, because Watts was likely to shove it up Spano's arse. No one stops or cares. I hear a couple of guys piss in the trees. They don't even bother to go walkabout. My legs are bouncing rubber. They've lost any connection to my body. It's a weird feeling to watch your legs walk away from you. I start singing, 'Wobble wobble wobble, the jelly's in trouble.' I'm delirious.

'Belt up, Knox.' I keep singing. The insults keep coming and I sing louder. 'You sound like crap.' 'If you don't shut up, there's no God.' 'Have you got a death wish?'

Then a couple of voices join in my singing. They've got to be delirious as well. We've all been up since four this morning, climbing mountains and taking shit.

'Jones, if we don't find this bloody cabin, you're going to die, Captain Bligh.'

I try to lighten it up. 'Mutiny on the bum, Jones.'

Jones actually has a sweat up. His Viking head is dotted with blobs. Maybe it's a nervous rash. 'I want to find the bloody cabin.'

'It's two bloody o'clock.'

'Just hang on, guys. It's only a little bit further.'

'Kill Jones.'

'Kill Jones.'

'Kill Jones.'

Flat land. We've bottomed out. The shit hole spade is in demand. A couple of guys have been holding on big-time. Three o'clock. My legs aren't rubber any more. There has been a meltdown. Glue. They don't bounce any more. Stuck to the ground. I've had it. 'If I'm going to die tomorrow, please God, let it be today.' I stop, waiting for lightning to strike me dead or a mud slide to bury me. Desperate. George slams into me like another glue pot. We're stuck together now. 'Jones,' I yell. 'Fuck the cabin.'

Suddenly the line wakes up. It's a chorus.

'Fuck the cabin.'

'Fuck the cabin.'

'Fuck the cabin.'

Jones has lost control here. I flash the torch at him. I actually see panic in those blue ice eyes.

'Right,' I shout. 'Find a spot. We're camping here.' Backpacks crash onto the ground. No argument. Groaning and moaning, bivvys are thrown anywhere and guys collapse under them.

Four o'clock. No cabin. The mountain stares down at us suckers. Torches off. Sleep.

CHAPTER 10

Seven o'clock. Wake up call. Eager beaver Seaten is banging George's dixie. 'Piss off,' spews from sleeping bags like a hangover morning. A cruel laugh echoes throughout the campsite. I open one groggy eye. It's Seaten. He's a zombie with his crazed red hair and pointy teeth. I'm hallucinating for sure and roll over.

'Morning. Sun's rising. Ready for the new day. Get up.' Bang, bang, bang. Seaten's fists pound the dixie cutting into my head like a scalpel. 'All right. All right.' Bang, bang, bang. I moan. I have to get up or I'll end up with a mashed brain. Voices grunt from under rocks and sticks. 'Come on! We're moving. Stop the bloody noise.' Sleeping bags worm along the ground. Guys slide out of sticky sleep into icy frost. I stretch out, give George a friendly kick and look around. Cold mist blankets the site in silent white. I try to grab the mist, but it's elusive. I take a deep breath and cough it out. I'm starting to smell. My gut spasms and I grab the shit hole spade instead. Calling out to Jones, I hold up the spade, then head inland.

A Willie wagtail pecks in front of me. Its tail is furiously moving from left to right in its excited search for the worm. How anything could be excited at this time of the morning is way beyond my brain capacity at the moment. 'Here Willie bird. Come here.' But you can never catch Willie wagtails because even though they are small, they're too fast and too smart. Not everything seems to be what it appears. I'm impressed with myself. Maybe I'm a philosopher? I laugh aloud. Or maybe just a bullshit artist.

The bush is thick and damp from the on-and-off rain of the past days. I have to twist between undergrowth and trees, careful not to slide on damp soil. The trunks seem connected in a chewing gum maze held together by woody lianas. It's become dank and dark. I'd have to be Tarzan to get through. I let out a heroic 'ah, ah, ooh, ohh' and frighten Willie away. I find a spongy spot to dig when I notice it — a sort of trail that lets in splintered light. I stop and squint at the light. I wonder where it leads? I hesitate. I have to get back to camp soon. Jones will be looking for me and I'm on hygiene detail. But it'll only take a few minutes to see where the trail goes. I won't follow it all the way.

The reddish rocky trail winds its way through the undergrowth breaking the liana stranglehold. There is a wombat hole. Big, fat, furry wombats. I saw one on the last trek with Andrew and Con. Miss those guys. Wonder what they are doing now? Con's sandwiches must be gone but Andrew's porno is probably doing its hundredth round. I crouch down to look at the wombat hole, but I don't disturb it. Wombats look cuddly, like fat-bummed koalas but if you pick one up they'll bite. Andrew found that out last time. He had to get a tetanus shot afterwards. He complained and hates wombats now. It was pretty funny. Wombats like to sleep. Me too. I'm going to sleep for a thousand years when I get home, if I ever get home. I stand and look around.

There's more trail. Better go back. Shit. I jump. Snake. No, no, I'm just getting the creeps. I kick the snaky branch away. The light is brighter just ahead. I've gone this far, should I go further? Maybe, just a bit further. Just to the light. The track is easier. The undergrowth is thinning, the dankness lessening. It's clearer, the mist lifting. Just a few more steps. I stand totally still. It's so quiet. I stare, then start to laugh and laugh.

The cabin. The cabin in all its glory. A roof. A floor. The river in front. Kangaroos grazing in the clearing. The kangaroos turn to gape at me. They think I'm mad or a giant kookaburra. Their noses twitch with the smell of me, then they thump away and I'm alone. I stand in the clearing for a while. Then I dig my hole in soft ground.

As I make it back to camp, I feel like Columbus returning with news that he has discovered America. 'I've found it.' I whistle. 'The place.'

'Right, Knox.' Guys jeer. 'Discovered the throne room have you?'

'Smart-arses. The cabin. I've found the cabin. Just ten minutes that way.'

'The cabin?' 'So why did we sleep on rocks last night?' 'Where was it?' 'Can't Jones read a bloody compass?' The complaining trickles into a flood, drowning Jones in swearing. Luke throws a handful of dirt at him. 'You've had it.' It's the signal. No one cares that they've had only three hours sleep, at least for now. It's rumble time with Jones as the target. There's tackling, wrestling, jumping and Jones is down. 'Give in? Give in?'

Jones raises his hands. 'I'm down.' Four bodies press him flat to the ground. George, Luke, Spano and Robbo peel themselves off him. He struggles up but he is grinning. 'Funny,' he mutters, brushing dirt from his shirt and his hair. Then he shakes his head like a dog splattering water and mud. 'Watch it, you mongrels.' Looking around, he gets his bearings. 'Had enough fun?' He then points in my direction. 'We're heading for the cabin.'

I head for breakfast first and just manage to grab a bowl of muesli before the gear is packed away. That's when Seaten gets me. Right in front of Watts's cooking bivvy, not that Watts does any cooking. Watts is smirking. 'No one goes out alone, Knox. You can get lost. Right?' Seaten has got to be kidding. As if I'd get lost in the bush? I'm not an idiot. I see Watts elbowing Robbo and they smirk together. Seaten is pathetic. Did he want to go with me and watch me shit? 'You have to give someone your bearings. Estimated time you're back.' I don't bother telling him that I'd told Jones. 'Getting lost out here is easy. Getting found is hard.' I don't answer Seaten. I just give him a snarling stare.

Spano thinks it's great. That ferret makes sure he's standing next to Seaten with a serious look when he nods his head agreeing. 'Knox could have got lost.' Spano gets under my skin.

The swearing is pretty creative as we look through the cabin checking out all the comforts we've missed. Most of it is aimed at Jones. Lucky he's Hercules because it bounces right off his muscle-bound chest not even shaking a hair.

It's another two hour trek along the river before we see the canoes. It is flat which is a bit of a relief, but you have to watch out for leeches. Hate those bloody things. Luke and Jones power ahead. Not me. I find a spot in the middle of the pack and pace myself. I'm feeling the after-effects of no sleep and sore leg muscles. There's a shout from Luke. The word 'canoes' runs down the line like electricity and everyone moves faster.

Canoes. That's not quite the right word for them. Scratched red and yellow plastic. They're just missing the nose rings. They look like they've been tripping and tripped right over a cliff.

'Only the best for us,' Luke yells, as he checks out one of them.

Sarah tries to look serious, but ends up laughing. 'A few of the other expeditions have given the canoes a rough time.'

'So they got the pre-sinkable types,' I answer. 'Save us the worry of keeping them afloat. We can just walk on water.' I look up to heaven. 'A religious experience.'

'Very funny. They'll float.' Sarah stamps the ground trying to demonstrate confidence. Her tits bounce and a couple of guys make some tit jokes. I reckon a few guys have the hots for her. Seaten, as well.

The river is about five metres wide. Downstream, we can see boulders jutting out creating swirlpools of white water. There has to be perch around those rocks, maybe trout as well. I stick my hand in the river. Cold. Maybe two or three degrees. Melting snow from the mountains feeds into it. A couple of guys flick each other with the ice water but no one is stupid enough to start a Sumo George wrestling match. No one wants their balls frozen off.

Seaten and Sarah are calling out from the river's edge. 'Over here.' Sarah pulls her hair back which means no jokes. 'Right, the rule of this expedition is that everyone has to prove they can swim in these waters. Some people lose their orientation because of the cold.'

'I can swim.' 'Like a dolphin.' 'Surfing champion.' 'Blood is made of ice. Don't feel the cold.'

'Great, guys. So you'll have no problems swimming here and now in this river. It's to test you in case your canoe overturns. For safety.'

'Safety? Everything will freeze off in that river. Important bits. You'll have a pack of girls for the rest of this expedition.' Luke scratches his black stubble, but not his balls. He'll have a beard for sure by the end of the week. 'We'll be racehorses without . . .' He reaches for his balls now.

I shove him, nod towards Sarah. 'Don't.'

Luke looks at Sarah who's trying not to smile. 'We'll be geldings.' He shoves his hands in his pockets. 'Is that okay?'

'Drowned geldings. I'm not doing it.'

'Me neither.'

'Want to remain a healthy male.'

Sarah ignores the protests. 'You have to swim from this side of the river and back. If you swim in your thermals, it'll keep you warm in and out of the water. It's early in the day so you will dry out pretty quickly.' She looks around. 'Who's first?' Dead silence. She nods at Jones hoping that if he makes the first move, the rest will follow. Not a movement. The freezing river has truly bonded us. We're not diving in. Seaten starts to push Spano towards the river. That's not fair, even if it is

Spano. Spano slips through his grasp. Good one. Hasn't Seaten heard of democracy? Oh shit, he's got him again.

'Come on, guys.' Sarah makes a face, then waits. Waits. She pulls her T-Shirt over her head and drops her shorts. She waits some more. I watch her. She looks lonely standing with her tits pointing out and her thermals gripping her body. Seaten stops pushing Spano. Everyone watches. Suddenly she plunges like an Antarctic icebreaker into the near frozen water and swims. The quick splashing of her arms cracks the air making her sound like a native bird. She's fast and furious reaching the other bank and back to our side of the river. Then she's out, her thermals clinging to her like a pornographic heroine. Watts grins adjusting his crotch. He says something to Robbo and they laugh. Dickheads.

Everyone is watching her. I look at Sarah standing there. Flashes cross my mind of how she crouched next to me overlooking the valleys and mountains. A shiver runs through me. I strip off my shorts and T-shirt, take a deep breath and jump in. The shock of cold blasts my balls into dried prunes. I have to swim and swim fast. The warmth of the thermals helps keep me breathing and my blood circulating. Then I hear splashes behind me. I do a turn passing Jones and Bennie. The rest following. Then I'm on shore again shivering, frozen.

We pass the swimming test and Seaten gets thrown in even though he doesn't have to do it. Seaten passes too. Wet and pretending to be angry, Seaten makes a fire and we all try to warm up.

Canoe preparation is serious business. Plastic watertight bags for our gear. Packing the most wet-sensitive stuff like sleeping bags into the driest section.

Paddles, canoe repair kit for leaks, drinking water. Then carefully balancing the canoe by putting backpacks and food provisions in the centre. Jones and I partner up. We check our canoe for cracks and holes. There are patches, but the repair jobs look sound.

Lunch is early. Another exciting round of crispbread and peanut butter. Sarah lectures us on white water canoeing. We've heard it all before. Then the camp is cleared. The rubbish is bagged and the fire stamped out. Estimated time on the river today. Five hours canoeing. We have to be off the river before nightfall. Too dangerous paddling in the dark. I'm looking forward to an early night sleeping on rocks next to farting Spano and snoring George. Desperate times. I smile to myself. At least Jones and I planned a food drop for tonight. Fresh meat for dinner. And our bivvy is on cooking detail. George and his dixie will be stars.

Seaten is the lead canoe, with Spano sitting behind him. Lucky Seaten. No one wanted to partner with Spano. He's light but he'll try and weasel out of paddling, and listening to him whinge for five hours could lead to murder on the river. Jones gets in the front of our canoe and I get in the back. Sarah pushes us off. 'Don't sink,' she jokes. I look over at George and Luke who are pushing their canoe in. It's already taking in water. It'll be cold sitting in a layer of water, but I guess the sun is out. They should survive. I'd be worried about the duct tape on their canoe. It doesn't look like it's holding too well, but it is the only canoe left. Take it or swim. A couple of the other canoes have taken George's and Luke's backpacks to lighten the load.

'I'll paddle on the right side,' I call out to Jones. He nods and takes the left side. We'll swap later. We start paddling. It will give my destroyed calf muscles a rest and I can work on destroying my arm muscles. The canoe rocks precariously from one side to the other. Balance isn't one of the strong features of this canoe and Jones and I are heavy guys. The threat of another frozen swim makes us work out our moves fairly quickly. In front of us is Seaten. He's obviously an expert. His canoe is gliding through the water like a duck. I start to laugh. Spano is paddling furiously. Poor little bastard. He'll have to do some work. Maybe Seaten isn't so bad. I point Spano out to Jones and he starts laughing too.

We keep veering left with every paddle. 'Jones, we're going to end up grounded on the left bank. Slow down.' Jones doesn't say anything. 'Remember, there's five hours of this. Let's survive.'

He thinks a while before answering, 'Okay,' and we slowly get our paddling rhythm. It is all right. No water pouring into the canoe. We're moving ahead. I can actually look around. A few water fowl are pecking at the riverside; funny looking birds with royal blue bibs. There's a smell of eucalyptus and the sharp whistles of butcher birds. Jones calls out, 'White water ahead.' We watch Seaten paddle around the rocks. Seaten is good and quick. If Seaten and weedy Spano can do it, so can we.

'Stop paddling, Knox.' Jones glances back at me before digging his oar into the water. I hold onto the sides of the canoe as we graze the rocks, splashing water into the boat, manoeuvring around the rocks. There's a drop and we yell. Round that boulder, down that dip. Wild. Jones's Viking arms bulge with muscles and strength. White water swirls, thumps and crashes.

Then we're back on quiet water. 'Good one, Jones.' I make a fist in the air. 'Let's go back and do it again,' I laugh.

'Wouldn't mind. Bad luck the river is going one way.'

We just start paddling again when there's shouting, and a cracking sound. A definite crack. We stop and turn around. George's canoe is down and even a Sumo can't hold a canoe full of river. It's sinking. Looks like the tape fell apart when they hit the white water. The rocks have broken the nose of their canoe as well. George and Luke are half swimming, half drowning as they drag the canoe to the riverbank. It must be bloody freezing. They are out of the water, jumping up and down like wet crazed fish. They scream out pointing at their canoe, 'Got to leave it. It's stuffed.'

Someone has to pick them up. We can't. We're too heavy. It'll have to be one of the canoes with a light man in it. It'll still be tough paddling with three. Hard to balance. Sarah collects George. Luke climbs into Bennie's canoe.

Rescue over. I feel the sweat roll down my back and I splash some ice water over me. The river ripples forwards and we start to paddle again, moving steadily through the brown-blue water. Jones and I give each other directions, paddle speeds, steering instructions until we instinctively know each other's moves. We wave to other canoes, laugh every now and then at Spano, who's still paddling, are quiet sometimes, talk other times. It's a relief from the pressure of the relentless trekking, pack activity and other guys.

'It'll be a long day tomorrow. All day on the river. Except for the portaging, which is worse.'

'That's tomorrow, Knox.'

My arms are already aching. 'The tide can take us for a while. Let's give paddling a rest. What do you think?'

Jones nods. I look at his arms glistening in the sun. They aren't aching or maybe he doesn't show it. He is Hercules. I tell him that, which makes him laugh.

'What do you think? I can fight the world?'

'I can't, but maybe you can. I like the way you stand up to Watts.'

'That jerk. Someone should put him down.'

I hesitate. 'Were you at that last Rave?'

Jones nods.

My skin crawls. 'Watts was there.'

'I saw him. Too much speed and vodka.'

'Did you see what happened in the toilets?'

'No, but I heard something afterwards. Trouble.'

'I think I saw it.'

Jones waits.

I want to say something. Explain about Watts and what I saw, but I can't. I haven't worked it out yet. I don't know why I tell him about my grandfather instead. 'He was in the Air Force. He knew how to fight. My grandfather taught me how to defend myself.'

Jones takes a long time to say anything. 'My father taught me never to back down.'

'Sometimes you have to back down.'

Jones rubs the blond stubble which is starting to look like a beard. 'There's never a reason good enough to back down for my father.' He squints into the sun. 'No. Never.'

'That's tough.' I feel my chest tightening. 'I don't have a father.' I wait for a while. 'But I had a grandfather.

He would have liked this river. He took me camping. Sometimes his Air Force mates would come with us. Grandpa taught me to fish. He'd wrestle with me sometimes.'

'You're lucky.'

'My grandfather died last year.' I can't speak after that. Jones somehow knows. I splash water over my head so that he can't see my face. He turns to look ahead.

CHAPTER 11

The eagles have landed. Well, we have. I walk like a barefoot ape that has just broken the pain barrier. My arms and legs are balanced now. Bow-legged, bow-armed, bow-brained. The only thing that saved me was partnering with Hercules. Jones dragged the canoe ashore by himself. My hands are too cut up. Blistered. 'Don't worry, Knox,' he'd said. I hung around and tied it up.

Spano is collapsed on his pack. There are sniggers. He can't even get Sarah to muster up any sympathy. George is organising the cooking. Thank God for the food drop. The sand is a bonus. George was so excited when he saw all the fresh food that he got right into it. His dixie is in full swing. He's belting out a specialty pot of fresh mince and tomatoes, which is much more important than all that jazz. Dixie and jazz. Ha, I'm a comedian or delirious again. George has plenty of energy to cook. He rode like a king in his canoe while the rest of us paddled and paddled. Five hours. George's canoe only had two paddles and three guys. No one would risk George tipping over the boat, so he didn't paddle. Sumo sunbaked.

Jones and I put up the tent. The ground is still damp from all that drizzle a few days ago. So it is easy to push in a few extra pegs to hold the tent. I slump down on the ground sheet, grab my backpack and fossick for my second pair of socks. Clean ones. I drag out my boots from my pack as well. Dry. Great. Rolling up the bottoms of my thermals is disgusting. They are caked with brown dirt. I pull the bottoms up slowly, when I suddenly see them. 'Shit,' I yell jumping up.

'Shit,' 'Shit,' 'Shit,' is being yelled from every direction.

Huge, bloated, black bloodsucking leeches have hit the expedition. 'Salt.' 'Salt.' 'Salt.'

George thinks fast and grabs handfuls of salt, pouring it into open hands. I get special George attention when he bypasses my cupped palms and chucks salt onto this monstrous blob on my leg. It drops off onto the ground like an amputated thumb. I'm shaking jelly. Hate leeches.

Sarah's shouting, 'Don't use salt, no salt.'

She's seriously losing it. 'It'll make the leeches suffer.' She grabs the bag of salt from George. 'Flick them off,' Sarah calls out. She is pointing to the leeches. 'Writhing in agony,' she claims. 'Salt dehydrates them.'

Dehydrating leeches are a real worry to me out here in the middle of bloody nowhere, with blistered hands and feet and Watts as company. I also care about mosquitoes. Sarah has got to be kidding. Dehydrating leeches. If they want to live, they should suck someone else's blood. Jones flicks his off. Spano does too, mainly because George didn't give him any salt and Sarah has confiscated the rest. Some use sticks to get them off leaving their suckers still in. They'll drop out after a while Sarah says. Watts is laughing. Others pound them into oblivion making blood ooze through their thermals. Blood and guts everywhere.

Shuddering, I rub my arms and legs. This is crazy. I check my legs. Nothing there any more. Everyone is running around in post-battle action — stripping down to skin checking for any missed bloodsuckers, assessing the damage before charging into the freezing river and dressing quickly. Then there is the sprint to the fire shivering until our teeth fall out or we get lockjaw. I've got the lockjaw. Too cold to even shiver. Luckily, Luke's group is on fire detail. That means there is plenty of wood and branches for the night, not like when Watts does it. 'Good fire, Luke,' I stutter. My arms are too frozen to wave. Slowly, I start to feel my toes and fingers. The smell of George's mince is drifting through the air and my lockjaw is turning into drooling.

'No leeches in the stew,' George shouts out. 'Dinner's on.'

No one even tells George to shut up. George is fast getting super-George status. A great cook, at least compared to the rest of us, and a great leech killer. Everyone is crazily blabbing about the massive leech invasion. I'm finally defrosted enough to move. I'm able to get up and help George. Jones does too. I won't let him. 'Hey, I'm doing your shift on cooking tonight.'

'Okay.' Jones nods. He's knows that's fair after his canoeing effort. I heap his bowl to the brim. He takes four slices of fresh bread. Who would have thought plain, unbuttered wholemeal bread could be so good? There won't be any more after tonight.

Sarah is giving a lecture on the value of leeches in the environment. I like Sarah but I think the environment has gone to her brain. Even Seaten has a smile on his face. I am definitely not interested in leeches and warn George to shut up when he mentions them.

George laughs. 'All right, all right. So what can I talk about?' He lumps stew into another bowl.

'Your cooking. Why do you know how to cook?'

George's face begins to glow and he starts swelling. It's a definite swell. Pride. He goes into great detail about the Italian restaurant his parents run. He works there after school and on weekends which is why he knows how to cook as well as eat. 'It's pretty hard work, but I can make every kind of pasta. Lasagne, fettuccine, spaghetti, tortellini . . .'

I elbow George in his side. 'George, I get it. You can really cook Italian.'

He beams. 'I can.' He tells me that he has a younger sister who helps out too. 'She can cook better than me. She's really good at it and my sister isn't fat.' I don't know why George tells me that his sister isn't fat and why it surprises me that he has a family and a life.

When everyone has had their dinner, George and I pile our bowls with leftover mince. 'Great food, George.' I nearly call him Fat George, but I don't. I'm not going to call him that again. 'George, this is great food.' He gets this satisfied smug look on his face and I have to punch him in the arm.

The cooking detail is completed. The dixie cleaned. Toilet dug. Disinfectant bowl and nailbrush set up. All tents pitched. The fire is blazing and it's only eight o'clock. It's the first time we've not been trudging through bush and ice at this time of night. Everyone is lounging around the fire, leaning on sleeping bags with their beanies pulled right down to their ears. There are a few jokes, kept fairly clean because of Sarah, a few last laughs about leeches, a bit of talk about tomorrow's canoe expedition.

'Remember, there's a mountain in between,' Sarah tells us.

'Great one.'

'Love those mountains.'

'Canoeing over trees sounds interesting.'

Joking turns to general talk. Sarah tells us that she's got a job as a National Park Ranger, but she's working on these expeditions to get experience and have fun before she starts. Luke can see the fun part, but then he is a freak of nature. He's into extreme sports like sky diving and leaping off tall buildings with a single bound. I can't see that George being stuck up the chimney, carrying Spano's gear, a snake up your arse, Watts being a bastard, or walking until you want to drop, as fun.

'It challenges you and you discover how much you can really do.' Sarah is serious. She pulls her hair back. 'Maybe you don't feel like it now, but afterwards when you think about it, you'll feel amazed at what you have done on this trip. It will empower you.'

Empower. I hate that word. It's the favourite teacher word at school. 'Empower yourself by studying, sports training, exploring your interests. You can achieve anything.' I look at Jones. Maybe he can, but everyone isn't Jones. And who wants to be? Was Grandpa? He just liked working with his hands, liked the bush, his mates, fishing, being home when I came back from school. I don't know what empowering means. I shiver.

'The chimney was a challenge. I bet you didn't think you could all do it?' Sarah warms her hands in front of the fire. Luke throws on some more wood. There's talk about the climb. Bennie has fallen asleep. Saliva is dribbling out of the corner of his mouth. Watts saunters away into the bush with the spade and torch, followed by Robbo and a couple of others. I guess it's a group shit.

Seaten gets up and walks over to Watts. 'You go by yourself and be back in a couple of minutes or I'll come and get you.' Maybe Seaten has worked out that Watts isn't really in love with the bush or needs to piss.

'Challenges have made people explore the unknown, uncover medical miracles, become great artists and writers or just find the best person inside themselves.' Sarah has this earnest look on her face. I don't know what she wants. I know that I don't want to be here. My stomach knots. I suddenly feel angry. Mum is at home. She's probably crying. I punch the ground. Little punches, then bigger ones.

Jones knocks my punch to the ground. 'Are you all right?'

I stop. Jones waits. 'I'm right. It's just been a long day.' I grimace. 'There's been quite a few long days.'

Jones nods.

I close my eyes for a moment, breathe in the eucalyptus air, block out the talk, listen to the bush rustling. Could be blue-tongue lizards scuttling between leaves or ring-tail possums climbing trees. 'Kwok, kwok, kwok' — currawongs. I can't see their yellow eyes and black-dagger bills in the dark. Big, black birds like crows. They breed in these mountains but survive nearly everywhere. Almost scavengers, they'll live in rubbish dumps if they have to. They eat birds' eggs and nestlings. Their beaks force hiding insects from under the bark of trees. They know how to stay alive. I hate them, but admire them.

There are swishing sounds in the air. I look up. Flying foxes? The moon is only a sliver tonight, with its light dulled by clouds. There are dark hollows in the mountain ridges where flying foxes wait for the night. I remember the first time I saw them. Grandpa and I had been camping near caves. It was nearly a full moon. They had come swooping out like vampires with black bat wings. I ran to Grandpa, hiding behind him. He hadn't laughed at me. He just held me. Later he told me that they come out at night looking for bush fruit and berries. Grandpa always explained the world to me and made me see my place in it.

Who needs challenges? Artificial challenges. Climbing these mountains to nowhere, descending into caves, for what? No, I just want to keep working at Pizza Palace. I want to earn enough money to buy Laura that gold bracelet. Laura. When I'm with her everything makes sense for a while. I just smell her hair, touch her skin, listen to her voice. Before I left for camp, she stayed late on the Saturday night. It had been amazing lying naked with her. She kissed me everywhere. I never thought she'd do that. I love Laura. I know I do.

Watts roams back. Robbo takes the spade. I rub my face, shake my head, glance up at Watts. Laura doesn't belong here. She's mine, not to share. I look at the fire. Through the flickering flames, I see George hugging his clean dixie. He's leaning his head against the cold metal. I shudder. I'll dream about Laura tonight. Warm dreams.

Seaten is talking about the cave. That bloody cave. 'You do the cave yourselves. Sarah and I will take your packs and be waiting when you come out. It's your big challenge.'

Seaten has got to be kidding.

'How do you get down?'

'What happens if you get stuck?'

'What about the underground river?'

'Are there snakes down there?'

'Is it dark?'

'Is there room to stand?'

Questions, questions, questions.

'What if you get stuck?' George reddens. 'I can't fit down a rabbit hole.'

'You'll have to stop eating, George, before we get there,' Watts laughs.

Watts is a rat. I'm going to beat him up one day. I don't need the cave and this garbage to find myself. Find my goals. Maybe that's what people need if they're Spano. Weaselly little weed. He needs a goal other than himself. He's been through nothing. I'm starting to hate Spano. I glare into the fire watching the flames burn. Grandpa's funeral was something.

Mum bought me a navy blue suit, blue shirt and tie. It was important to her. Mum was always very careful with money, not because she was mean. It's just that she wanted to save enough so that we could go away on a week's holiday every year. Somewhere special. She tried to pay for Grandpa, but he never let her. She put other money aside as well. In case of emergencies. If we didn't need it, she'd save it for my education. She hated taking money from Grandpa. 'He spends enough on both of us.' Grandpa bought me my fishing rod and goalie gloves for soccer. He bought Mum her little second-hand car. He knew what was important and would buy things without us asking.

Mum didn't want to save any money on my navy blue suit. We went to the best menswear shop. She asked for the finest suit, finest shirt, finest tie. It cost a lot, but Mum didn't care. She was crying as we left the shop and I had a rock in my throat.

Mum didn't want the most expensive coffin in the funeral parlour. 'He wouldn't have liked that one.' I agreed. It was decorated with fancy designs and gold-plated handles. I was proud when Mum asked me to choose the coffin. I looked for a long time before I found the one. It was plain. The wood was highly polished with a greyish tinge like gums. Grandpa loved the huge gums that lined the banks of inland rivers. The coffin had wooden handles. I wanted to put some eucalyptus leaves inside the coffin so Grandpa would not forget the scent. I looked at the funeral director in his black suit and serious manner. I was afraid to ask him. But this was not about me. It was for Grandpa. I asked. The funeral director said, 'Of course,' and I felt stupid.

The black funeral hearse was filled with flowers. Mum had bought a wreath of yellow wattles, red banksia, waratahs. The wreath was on the top of the coffin. There were so many people at the Chapel. Grandpa's work friends, the Christos's, Andrew with his mother, Con with his parents, Grandpa's war mates, strangers and friends. I stood next to Mum, looking at the ground.

Four men in Air Force uniform carried the coffin into the Chapel in the crematorium. I looked up and saw their ribbons pinned onto their suits. Grandpa had medals. They were mine now. They were in my pocket.

I knew about crematoriums. Crematoriums were for burning. I looked over at the Navigator. His face was scarred with burns. Why was Grandpa here? Why were we here? Grandpa had become very thin in the end. He didn't eat in the end. In the war, Grandpa's plane had been shot down in flames. Why was Grandpa here?

I stared at the old veterans. Suddenly I grabbed onto Grandpa's medals as pain tore through me. 'Mum, have to go. Toilet.' I ran to the bathroom, dry retching into the bowl until green bile stung my nose and throat. I washed my face in the basin, then looked into the mirror. 'Grandpa, you promised. You promised you wouldn't leave us until we didn't need you any more.' I whispered. 'I need you.'

Grandpa was going to be burnt until he was ashes. I would never see him again.

CHAPTER 12

Day five. I lie on my back waiting for morning. I listen to George's laboured breathing and turn to look at him. His face is sunburnt and peeling. This camp has been tough for George. His body is made for comfort not for speed. I gave him some talc to reduce the chaffing between his legs. I was glad that he didn't canoe yesterday. His hands are too blistered. Worse than mine. George needed to get fit before starting this 'challenge'. Bloody challenge. George has never even played soccer. Can you believe that he admires me for being goalie for the Mighty D's? George admitted to me that he'd never played in a real team for soccer or football or any sport. When he was little, his parents couldn't take him to the games because they were working too hard. Later, George had to work in the restaurant. He's never been on a holiday either, except he once stayed overnight at a motel for a cousin's wedding. He wasn't angry about any of it though.

George told me that his father had come to Australia from Italy with nothing. He'd married an Australian girl, worked hard to set up Café Piazza Italia, looked after his family and bought a house last year. 'We don't live over the restaurant any more. I have my own bedroom now.' When George told me that, he glowed like a bursting tomato.

I have always had my own bedroom and Mum cooking dinner and Grandpa always took me to play soccer on Saturday mornings and I have gone on a holiday every year for as long as I can remember.

I glance at sleeping Jones. He looks like a statue lying on a crypt, except his beard is curly blond and growing. Jones actually told me yesterday, after three hours of paddling, that his father is an engineer who builds multi-storey buildings and that his mother is a dentist. It's one of the few personal things he has told me. I was half shocked that he actually has real parents and they do something. I was starting to think he came from a pod, planted by aliens in a frozen Viking glacier. Jones is starting to move. I smile. It's like watching an animated movie. Marble is turning into human form. Jones opens his eyes. They are piercingly blue and focussed.

Nearly five o'clock. The camp is getting up, the daily routine beginning. Packing, hygiene, rubbish, site clearance, water bottles, breakfast. I roll up my sleeping bag. George is rumbling. Spano isn't. We've given up asking, punching, harassing Spano to help. He's won. He does nothing. It was great watching Seaten force him to work the canoe yesterday. Seaten actually made me happy for once.

I look around and see Seaten stomping over to our bivvy. That weasel Spano notices too and ducks for cover into his sleeping bag. Seaten drags Spano's sleeping bag down around his neck. He says with a straight face, 'Then you're right for canoeing today.

You're teaming up with me again.' Spano tries to object, but Seaten has turned away from him. He winks at me. A definite wink.

There is a group meeting before the canoeing starts. Sarah is doing a head count, and everyone is inspecting gear and making sure the canoes won't sink. Jones is explaining the route. It will be about four hours paddling before we reach the mountain. Sarah says it's only a hill but I know that after all that paddling, it won't seem like that. Then there will be more paddling. By the end of the day, our arms will have dropped off and we'll get to camp and have to eat dinner with our feet.

Sarah is doing a final body count. 'Bennie?' No answer. 'Bennie?'

A few of the guys call out, 'Where are you, you moron?' 'Come on.' 'Bloody get your act together.' Bennie has been losing it in the last couple of days. He fell badly at the chimney. No one talks to Bennie, except to laugh at him, give him a few shoves.

Sarah shouts out. 'Someone look for Bennie. We're not going until he's found.'

There is moaning. We want to get going. 'I saw him out the back. There . . .' Luke points into the bush. He doesn't wait for anyone and sprints across the campsite. Luke always runs. He's got so much energy that he's jumping out of his skin most of the time.

'Make it fast,' Seaten shouts out to Luke. 'Bennie is an idiot.'

'Sure.' Luke is gone.

Everyone agrees that Bennie is an idiot, then we just hang around and wait. Cut hands, sunburnt faces, torn muscles, tiredness, make us edgy. Sarah says we have to wait until Luke gets back or 'You'll all end up running around in circles and we'll never get onto the river.' The waiting is bad. Everyone knows starting late will mean extra pressure to paddle faster. We'll be late getting to the mountain, late climbing it, late getting back in the canoe and late to camp.

It only takes five minutes before it starts — jumpy comments, flicking stones, slouching hard shoulders against trees. Bennie had better be back soon. Ten minutes. Swearing. Twenty minutes. Kicking trees. Half an hour. Murder.

Luke's got him. 'Fallen into a ditch,' he shouts. 'He's all right. Knees grazed, that's it.' Murder has to wait. We've got to get moving. Strap our helmets on. Canoes hit the water. The river is freezing. Jones and I shove off. My muscles tear into action. The pain. I ignore it, not because I'm brave, but what's the point? No one is going to save me. Not here anyway. The canoeing is fast. Spano and Seaten lead the pack. Jones and I are paddling quickly. I peer back to shore checking how far we have paddled. Bennie is getting into a canoe. A rock flies through the air. Bennie ducks so that it just misses him.

'Jones, look around. At the shore.' I point to Bennie.

Jones squints back. There is another rock. It hits Bennie. Hard.

We paddle for a while with the water lapping at the sides of the canoe. The banks are dense with gums. Reeds edge into the river. A small water dragon skims through them. A prehistoric leftover from the dinosaur age. Then Jones says, 'Bennie is too slow. Even slower than George.'

'He wants to go home. But he's not like Spano. It's just too difficult for him.'

'He's slowing down the trek, Knox. He's got everyone offside. His bivvy group isn't a great help.' His face becomes hard. 'Watts.'

We purposely avoid mentioning the throwing of the rocks. It's too complicated to understand. And if we do understand, what does it make us?

'He cut himself pretty badly at the chimney. Hard to believe he could fall off that ridge.'

'They'll send him back if he has a broken leg.'

'He'd better break it soon, because someone is going to kill him.'

Watts. He'll kill someone. But it's not only Watts any more. Bennie has become a target. 'I think he's throwing himself down gullies on purpose.' I jolt forwards as I push my paddle hard into the water. Am I supposed to do something? I can hardly make it through this myself. What?

What should I have done at the Rave?

Watts pulled Annie's top off so that her tits were exposed. His fingers were squeezing them. The veins stuck out from the back of his hands like caterpillars and they left red imprints on the whiteness of her skin. She was sobbing, 'No, no, no . . .' until it was drowned out by the noise of everyone cheering, banging the stainless steel urinals. Then he put his hand over her mouth.

I don't know if other guys jumped on her afterwards. I don't know when it stopped. I climbed down from the broken ladder and leant against the laneway wall with the stinking garbage and then I vomited.

What should I have done?

* * *

The rhythm of the paddles has a hypnotic effort. We move smoothly along the river and, except for the aching of my arms, it is calm. I'm glad Jones doesn't talk. If Andrew was here, he'd talk. We talked after the Rave. Andrew hadn't seen it like I had, but he knew what happened. He said we weren't involved. It was Watts's problem. I was relieved. Annie never reported it. She was afraid. Watts promised to break anyone's legs if they reported it. Afterwards there was argument and bravado and excuses by a lot of people. In the end there were only whispers and Annie left her school. After that, I didn't say anything. No one did. How could we? We'd watched or cheered or had been part of it. How could you tell anyone? I wanted to believe Andrew. Not my responsibility. I couldn't speak to Mum about it because she hardly smiled any more. I needed to ask Grandpa, but he was dead.

Afterwards, Andrew got his nipples pierced. It was at a shop at the beach in between the tattoo art and the ice-cream shop. There were a lot of kids around in gothic black with pierced eyebrows and earlobes and tongues. But Andrew was drooling over the beach girl in a small orange bikini and g-string. She was getting a nose stud. It only took a few seconds and she smiled when she looked in the mirror and saw the silver stud in her nose. Andrew chatted her up. 'You look great,' he said as he lay on the couch. 'Nipples,' he said. He screamed when the body artist stuck the needle right through his nipple. The girl with the nose stud left with a surfer in board shorts and a tattoo of a shark on his arm.

After his nipple had been pierced, I lay back on the vinyl covered bench.

I closed my eyes, clenched my fingers into the palms of my hands until the nails dug red lines into them. The attractive blonde girl leaned over me, brushing my nipple with antiseptic. It was cool. Her long hair tickled my chest. 'Is your name Annie?' I asked.

She shook her head, her hair tickling my chest again. She swept it back with one hand rolling it like a sausage to the side of her head. The metal clamp was hard. I didn't like the pressure. The hollow stainless needle pierced through my nipple. The pain was sharp, burning, terrible. My body went into spasm as she pressed it through to the other side. She put a metal ring through it. Then she did the other nipple.

I am a coward. I should have done something. I took the metal nipple rings out after a week. There was no point to them. Andrew still has his.

Jones calls out to me. I force myself to focus. He motions to a muddy inlet. Canoes have landed there already. I can see Seaten pulling in his boat and Spano collapsed on the bank. I take my paddle out of the water while Jones steers the canoe towards shore. Then we both start paddling fast, crossing the current to the landing.

Jumping into the freezing water, and pushing the canoe onto the mud is a relief. The sun is glaring. There's cold splashing. All the boats pull in and are dragged to shore and then we look up. The mountain–hill. There are scattered trees on it, but it's mainly long dry grasses like a sea of straw. Luke runs barefoot up to the foothill to assess the terrain, then he runs back mighty quickly. 'Bloody grass. Like knives.' His feet are lined with thin cuts. He yells out, 'And there are snakes. Brown. Lots.'

Everyone stops. Boots on, thermals down. I squint. It's going to be hard work getting the boats up to the top, but there's only one way out of here. Up. Jones and I lift our canoe onto our shoulders, but we don't last long. Too heavy, even for Jones. Too heavy for everyone. Canoes drop like flies. Only wish they would. The flies are landing in battalions as we shove these lead-weight canoes through the grasses. My hands are cut to pieces. The sweat is dripping down my face. Luke risks swallowing a fly colony and starts with his jokes.

'What is brown and sticky?'

'Shit, like this.'

Luke's laughing. 'A snake up your arse.'

'Good one, Luke.'

'How do you know nearly everyone here has sex on the brain?' That's an Andrew question for sure. 'Because you're all dickheads.'

Bennie is struggling behind me. 'Move it, Bennie.' There is a cut above his eye. Flies have landed on the drying blood. 'How is it going?' I call out. No answer. 'Bennie, how is it going?'

He shrugs. 'Good,' he mutters under his breath.

George has had it. 'Luke, look at that.' I'm laughing. Luke is laughing too. George is lying flat on his back in the long grass, puffing and panting. He's red and big and planted and he's not going anywhere. You can see his left foot, his fat head and the dixie sticking out beside him from the grasses. Luke is threatening him with a punch up if he doesn't move. George refuses. Sumo is stuffed.

He's hugging his dixie and staying put. Even superman Luke can't get the canoe to the top by himself. 'That's it. You're dead meat. Push the canoe or I'll stomp you.'

George shakes his head. 'No way.'

Luke is getting ready to give George a big kick when Sarah steps in. She whispers something in George's ear. My God, does he move. The dixie is thrown into the boat and George is pushing. Luke can't believe it, but doesn't stop to question why.

It takes two hours and forty-five minutes to land the boats on the hilltop. Sweating, starving, stuffed; bodies, boats and oars lie like a post-war battlefield. A couple of commanders like Jones and Luke check for life and throw a few water bottles around to desperate casualties.

Luke is on cooking and distributes Vegemite and crispbreads. 'Thought you might be sick of peanut butter.' Sarah is sitting looking down at the river bend on the other side. I slump on the ground next to her and hand her the crispbreads. I have to ask her. 'What did you say to George?'

She smiles. 'Snakes.'

'He knew that already.'

'He didn't like the one I said was sliding up his pants.'

We laugh.

CHAPTER 13

It is downhill now. Red and yellow canoes flash through the grasses and over bushes. Canoes are sliding at greater and greater speed down the hill. Robbo is screaming, 'Move out of the way.' He's in his canoe trying to white-water raft grass and trees. Watts is powering after him egging him on.'Go, Robbo, go.'

'Get out of that canoe,' Seaten is yelling at Robbo.

Too late. Crash. Robbo is out of the canoe now. Face down in dirt with the canoe's nose flattened against a tree. Another Rave guy hits the dust. That canoe is not going to party anywhere for a while.

Jones and I are running after our canoe. Jones has nearly caught it. No, it's going to hit George.'Get out of the way, George.' George turns around like a cabbage ready to be chopped. 'Jump, George, jump.' Just in time.

Canoes slicing snakes to pieces, screeching birds escaping, skinks running for cover under rocks, racing adrenaline. It's fast, furious and fun. Thirty minutes downhill and we've landed.

Seaten inspects Robbo and Watts's flat-nosed canoe. 'Have to leave it here. It'll sink on the river,' Seaten barks at Robbo. 'That ride down the hill was pretty stupid. Maybe the canoe can be repaired. It'll have to be collected.' He shakes his head. 'You look like you need a bit of repair too.' Robbo can hardly hold his head up. His nose is scraped raw and his ear is swollen and blue. 'We won't leave you here to be collected. The expedition organisers might not be impressed with your roller coaster.'

Everyone is down from the top now with canoes and jumbled gear. That was wild portaging. A great ride. 'Repack and check your boats,' Sarah calls out. 'Then get onto the river.'

It's a wider stretch of water than the other section, and deeper. Less visible rocks. There is a bit of white water but not too serious. Seaten is the leader. Canoes dot the river behind him. Jones gets a burst of energy and we glide past Robbo who was offloaded into Sarah's canoe. She runs the hospital ship. Bennie is on it too. Lucky Sarah. I wave at her. She waves back.

We catch up to Seaten's canoe and paddle alongside it for a while. Spano, Watts, Seaten. 'They look like a happy team, don't they?'

Jones smiles. Watts was ordered into Seaten's boat. He is at the front snarling like a jackal, while Spano is at the back paddling like a frenzied flea. The sun hits Seaten's hair, blinding us with its reddish streaks. His hair matches his face, beaming like an orange ready to squirt Watts and Spano in the eye if they stop paddling.

We let them streak ahead, slowing our pace to rest our arms and blistered hands for a while. 'Water.' I throw Jones a bottle. Then I take my iodine water bottle out and drink as well. It's quiet along the river. I point to two water dragons sunbaking on the bank. Jones looks over at them. We take our time drinking our water, watching the dragons, the river. Jones motions to my paddle. 'Better get moving.' We start again.

Rainbow lorikeets wing past. Lorikeets remind me of home. They visit our backyard every afternoon. Grandpa built a bird bath for them near the workshop. Mum leaves seeds out, but lorikeets love sugar. It's not good for them. Sometimes I pour sugar into my hands and stand on the back porch. They dive for it flapping their bright green wings. Dozens of them. Their red beaks nibble my hands while their blue-feathered heads bob up and down like corks. They land on my arms or shoulders or head, walking on me as if I'm a perch. There is this strange feeling I get when they do that. They trust me.

Trust. I shudder. Lately things seem confused. I've been doing things. It was Andrew's idea to steal the STOP road sign. I didn't keep it. Andrew wanted it. I lied to Mum and said I was just going for a bike ride. That night I helped Andrew unbolt the road sign and I cut myself on one of those stupid bolts. It was rusty. I could have got tetanus. I didn't, but I would never have told Mum even if I did get tetanus. Andrew already had two road signs in his bedroom. He didn't need another one. With no STOP sign on that street, there could be car accidents. I hate going past that street. The road and transport people should replace it. I wanted to tell Mum what I did but she would have been angry. It would have hurt her too. I couldn't tell her about it. We don't talk very much any more. I didn't tell her about the camping trip.

It was two weeks after the funeral. It had been raining for a week when the first day of sunshine broke through the weather pattern. Andrew had been waiting for the rain to stop for our great camping trip. Con, Andrew and me. I didn't want to go on it, but Mum insisted. 'You just enjoy the camping trip. Nothing has changed.'

'Mum, I don't really want to go.'

She shook her head. 'I know you do. You love camping. Grandpa always went camping with you. Nothing has changed,' she said. That was untrue. Everything had changed.

Con beeped the horn. He had just passed his driving test. He was seventeen now with a licence and a car. He'd used all his birthday and Christmas presents to buy it. (Greeks always seem to give money, lucky for Con. His parents didn't let him spend it until now, which is again lucky for Con.) His father went with him to check out the second-hand market. They argued and argued over which car Con should buy. His father wanted Con to buy an old Volvo, built for safety and size. A family of five would have loved it. Con wanted to buy a converted Chevrolet with a double exhaust and speakers built into the doors.

They compromised. Con bought a twelve-year-old blue panel van. A great car. It has everything a guy could want — power and acceleration with an eight-cylinder engine, a making-out area with double mattress and pillows at the back, and plenty of storage for camping and surfing gear. Con spent three weekends working on it, touching up scratches, filling in dents, waxing and polishing it. The final touches were the yellow signs hanging from the back window — 'Breast Testing Unit', 'Hotmobile', 'Chicks Welcome'.

The camping gear was thrown into the back and I squeezed into the front bench next to Andrew. I told Mum that Con was a safe and responsible driver. She'd been nervous. 'I don't want anything to happen to you . . .' Mum didn't finish. She wanted to say, now that Grandpa is gone.

Her pale face was etched with barely controlled pain. I closed my eyes because I didn't want to see it. She waved goodbye. As Con turned the corner, he turned the radio on full blast. Then he slammed his foot down on the accelerator spinning the van into a loop. We shouted at him to slow down. But no. Leadfoot drove like a psycho-out-of-hell all the way to the National Park.

We got out of the car shell-shocked. Con stretched his arms when we jumped him, flattening him onto the ground. Con fought, but his arms were pinned. 'What are you doing, guys?' he spluttered.

'Drive like that again and I'll smash you.' Andrew thumped his stomach.

'Hey, that hurt.'

'Con, you're insane in the car.' I thumped Con too.

'I'm not and stop hitting me.'

Andrew knuckled Con's arm. 'You need sex. Too many Greek family parties and not enough action. Forget driving. Sex.'

'As if you're getting any?' Con kicked his legs around trying to get up. I sat on them.

Andrew laughed. 'I had a pretty good night with Angela. She's hot.'

'Shut up about Angela.' I rolled Andrew. 'You were so drunk and disgusting.'

Con jumped up and did a flying leap onto Andrew and we rumbled in the dirt until we were too tired to rumble any more. We lay on our backs trying to get back our breath.

Andrew was the first up. 'Okay, let's move. Can't lie about all day,' Andrew said. 'I have a plan.' That sounded like trouble.

We staked out our site, pitched the tent, set up the fireplace. Then back into Con's panel van. 'Con, take your foot off the accelerator or you're dead.' Andrew pretended to stab Con.

'Funny. Very funny.'

We drove out of the National Park inland along the main highway. Leadfoot was starting to accelerate again, when Andrew pointed to a dirt road. 'That way.'

Con's eyes lit up in this strange demonic way. Dirt road, no cars, no police. Con let out a yahoo and veered to the right, screeching the wheels of the panel van. He belted down that dirt road burning rubber, spitting rocks behind us like a volcanic eruption. 'Slow down you bloody idiot,' Andrew yelled in his ear. Greek boy cuts loose — there was no way Con was slowing down.

'We're here, we're here,' Andrew screamed.

Con slammed on the brakes and we would have gone through the windscreen except for our seat belts. Con was laughing. Andrew had his hands around his neck and I threw myself across their bodies to grab the key.

We fell out of the van onto the road to nowhere. We were in the middle of fields that went on as far as you could see. No houses, no people, just fat brown and white cows grazing. A couple of cows looked up at us with their big brown eyes, then went back to eating. Low wire fences and a ditch separated the road from the fields in some places. There were no fences in other parts.

Andrew took out a plastic bucket from the back of the van. 'Follow me.' We jumped across the ditch, then climbed the fence.

'Isn't this private property?' I looked at Andrew. 'Farmers use shotguns for trespassers, don't they?'

Andrew laughed. The soil was still damp from the rain with muddy patches. 'Find cow dung. The bigger the cowpat, the better.'

'Are we looking for shit?' I asked.

'Yes, shit. Magic mushroom shit.'

The mushrooms were golden bronze with white stems growing on black cow dung. Andrew and Con found a few. As I pulled one out, its stem turned bluey-black. The cows mooed. Con stepped in a big cowpat. As Andrew laughed, he looked up and saw a truck heading across the field. 'Farmer,' Andrew shouted. 'Run.' He grabbed the bucket and we ran across the fields, past the cows, through the grass, with the farmer's truck closing in.

'Shotgun,' I shouted. We ran faster. Over the fence, into the ditch, piling into the van. I jumped into the driver's seat, started it and slammed my foot on the pedal. With Con hanging halfway out of the car we made our getaway.

Finally, we got back to our campsite. I was shaking. Con didn't look so great either. 'Lucky the police didn't stop us. I've got no licence.'

'Criminal,' Andrew laughed, but he was shaking as well.

'That was close.' Con pretended to shoot Andrew.

We collapsed for a while, letting the adrenaline gradually fade. We joked about the close call. 'The gun, the run, the fun.' Andrew summed it up.

'Don't know about the fun.' I shook my head.

'Okay, let's go.' Andrew got up. We followed. We gathered sticks and bark and lit the campfire. Andrew held the frying pan over the flames.

'How do you know these aren't toadstools? Poisonous?'

Andrew flipped the mushrooms. 'My brother let me tag along with his college mates the last time he went out. Most are poisonous. They'll kill you, but these are all right.'

'So you've been out once and you know all about them?'

'I know enough.'

'For us to die.' Con shakes his head. 'Your mum would ground you forever if she knew about this.'

'Well, she doesn't know, does she?' Andrew and his mother were always arguing. She phoned our place a few times looking for him when he didn't come home. He'd slept at a mate's place without telling her. I couldn't do that. 'What she doesn't know, doesn't hurt her.'

'Heard Watts and some guys did magic mushrooms a couple of weeks ago. They went off their faces.' Con was serious.

'Yeah, but you know Watts. He did four or five mushrooms, alcohol and who knows what else.'

'He thought he could fly. He was going to jump off the cliffs at the Heads, except Robbo saved him.'

'That's bad luck. Watts over a cliff sounds good.' Andrew's voice was getting annoyed.

'Okay, who wants to go first?'

'I'm not doing this.' Con folded his arms in front of him.

'They aren't real drugs. It's just for fun. It takes you on a trip. That's it.'

Con shakes his head.

'What is it? Your Greek mummy and daddy wouldn't like it?' Andrew pierced a mushroom with his fork and offered it to Con. 'Come on. Have it.'

'Don't want it.' Con pressed his lips together.

'Go on.' Andrew was starting to really hassle. 'Go on. Wimp. Go on.'

'Shut up, Andrew.' I threw a stick at him. 'Hey, Con can do what he wants.'

Andrew spent two hours floating between laughing and great insights. He'd found the meaning of life. God was the frying pan. Couldn't we see it? The world was a great pot and we were the ingredients that made the cake.

'You're a cake. A nut cake,' Con laughed, but Andrew was serious, wanting us to see the light. The frying pan was God.

It took a while for the mushrooms to work on me. I focussed on Andrew's insights about the frying pan, then went beyond them into the fire. The yellows and reds of the flames fascinated me, growing and shrinking like hands. Suddenly they were Watts's hands pulling me into this fire, distorting skin and blond hair. I was burnt and screaming. Con said that I sobbed for hours, finally crawling into the tent and sleeping it off. I remember the crying. I don't understand it, but I remember.

I never told Mum the truth about the camping trip. She asked me about it. She trusted me. I told her that I had a good time. I lied.

CHAPTER 14

Five days trekking without showers, toilets, beds, clean clothes, with no real friends. I've lost a lot of weight. Everyone has. Our canoes are beached and everyone is setting up camp for the night. Jones motions to me that he's secured the rope on one side of our bivvy. George is doing the other. I check the A-frame knots. Spano isn't around. I call out to Jones and George, 'Right.' Jones gives the rope an extra tug. 'Good one.' I look at them. 'Okay.'

'We're on water.' Jones grabs his empty water bottle.

George beams. 'The river is right in front of us.'

'Everyone has to have one good day.' Jones goes to collect the camp bottles.

Even with sore shoulders and cut hands, I manage to throw everything out of Spano's pack to get the iodine. It has become one of those sadistic rituals that I really enjoy. He'll come back and whinge and Jones will say with a straight face, 'Knox had a hard time finding the iodine. Bottom of the pack.'

'It wasn't. It wasn't,' Spano will answer. 'I left it right on the top.'

'Knox, you had better be more careful next time.' Jones will say, still with a serious face.

Camp dinner is quieter than usual. The cave is on everyone's minds. I look around. Bennie is sitting by himself. His plastic bowl is still full. He doesn't eat. George is up to his second bowl. Jones has the compass out. The cave is north. Half a day's trek inland. He's staring in that direction.

Watts is sitting next to Seaten, looking ratty. Seaten caught him with alcohol the other night. He wanted to send him back. 'But only after the cave,' he said. 'Don't want you to miss out on that Watts.' He'll get suspended for sure. Robbo is at a loose end now and has been hanging around Luke. Robbo is one of those guys who needs to follow someone. Luke could lead Robbo up a cliff or into a volcano, but at least Luke won't send him into the volcano by himself. There may be hope for Robbo.

Dinner finishes and our final briefing for the cave begins. 'You'll be on your own. There will be no one handing out ointment and sympathy.' Seaten gives a smart-arse look at Sarah. Now I remember why I hate him.

She raises her eyebrows and places her hands over her heart. 'Call me Nurse Kindness.' There is laughing and a few jokes about nurses and how we all need special attention. Female, of course.

'All right, all right. Settle down.' Seaten glares at Sarah. He never seems to get one over her. 'First, there's the drop.' There are still snickers about nurses and bedside care. 'Are you listening? Is this funny?' The jokes stop. 'You jump into the hole one by one. You wear your helmet. Saves cracked skulls.' He smirks at each one of us. 'And by the way, the snakes aren't in the cave, they're up here.' He looks at Watts, then waits a few seconds before continuing. 'When you land inside the cave, you have to shout up the hole for the next one in line to jump. Make sure you've moved out of the way before the next one is down. That is, unless you'd enjoy someone like Fat George landing on your head.'

Why doesn't Seaten grow up? Something should land on his head. There's a bit of sniggering. 'Sumo George could make a few guys into meatheads.'

'There are plenty of meatheads here already,' George back answers.

'Once you're down, it's too low to stand. There could be mud from all that rain last week as well. You crawl along in line. Foot to head. Foot to head. It's dark, but you'll have torches. Watch out for the stalactites and stalagmites. There will be passages. Some of them dead ends. There's another cave. It's the wrong way. There are bats in that one but they won't hurt you. You'll have to send scouts ahead. There is only one passage out.'

'Who leads?' George's face is flushed.

Seaten glances around. 'You have to work out who you want to lead.'

Voices call out Jones' name. He stares at Seaten with no expression on his face.

'Once you reach the cave you'll know it. There is an underground river. It makes a pool in the cave. You dive into the pool and you'll feel the rock wall under the water. It's cold.'

'How cold?' Luke asks.

'Freezing.' Seaten waits for that to settle in. 'There's an opening in the wall under the water. Climb through it, then surface in the river. It's warmer than the cave. You're out then. Sarah and I will be waiting with your gear.'

'Well, that sounds easy,' Luke says sarcastically.

Seaten laughs. 'It's not too bad,' but everyone knows that is untrue.

We're worried as we wander off to our tents for an early night. 'So, Jones, what do you think?'

'Should be all right.'

'It's dark down there.' I point to the ground. 'Have you done anything like this before?'

It takes him a while to answer. 'My father took me onto one of his building sites when I was eight. It was a site on water. We went under the pylons. There was lots of mud. It was dark.' He hesitates. 'There were rats.'

I wait for Jones to go on. He doesn't. 'So your father and you do a lot of things together?'

'No, I didn't say that.' He hesitates again. 'He has always taken me to his building sites. He's made me climb scaffolding where people looked like beetles on the ground or under pylons where you can't see.'

'Weren't you scared?'

'You just have to do it. He wants me to be an engineer like him.'

'Do you want to?'

'No.'

It is like drawing blood out of brick. 'Was it all right under the pylons?'

'No.'

Jones scratches his beard methodically, concentrating on thoughts in his head. I rub my face. My beard is fuzzy. I break the silence. 'My grandfather was a carpenter.'

Jones blinks as though he's surprised I'm still here.

'I liked working with him. Maybe I'll do that when I leave school. All his tools are still in his workshop at home.' Suddenly my arm goosebumps into tingles and spiders.

Jones and I walk to our tent without speaking. Jones points to the bush. 'Need a piss.' He leaves, disappearing into scrub and bushes. I drag out my sleeping bag, then wander off to find a place to be by myself. I discover a spot hidden behind gum trees. Grandpa's sleeping bag is heavy. I spread it out and slot myself inside it. Then I just lie there, listening to the bush sounds, staring at the stars. The last time I was in Grandpa's workshop was before he was sick. We'd been working on a surprise for Mum. A glory box, Grandpa called it. 'It's for her to keep her special things.' He talked about the war, that last time. Lately, things were making him think about it, he had said. Maybe it was because he was getting older, or maybe because he knew he was sick. He'd been seeing more of his war mates, the ones who were still left. He'd meet them for a beer in the evenings sometimes. He saw a lot of the Navigator.

Grandpa had been a bit older than I am now when he went to war. Only the very best were accepted in the Air Force. Grandpa was one of the best. Squadron 460 stationed in England. He flew 30 missions into Germany. He was only twenty years old. Grandpa said that half the airmen didn't come home.

'Lancasters. They could really fly. More than 4,000 kilometres in one go, carrying a 7,000 pound bomb load. Lancs. They were fast. 460 kilometres per hour. That might not seem fast to you, Sam, but it was then.' Grandpa had

told me about his famous Lancs before — the airmen, their missions, air battles. Sometimes he repeated himself but he always added something new, explained something more. 'We could go higher than 24,000 feet.' He moved back and forth, sanding the glory box smooth. 'Not much higher than that.' He stopped to look at the smoothness of his work. I ran my hand over it. 'There were always three gunners. The tail gunner, I was one of them, sitting in a perspex bubble at the rear of the plane with a machine gun. The gunners were the first target. Had to knock us out. The noise was deafening.' Grandpa waited. He looked at me for a while. 'I want to tell you this, because I didn't know it when I was a boy back then.' He pointed to the familiar old black and white photograph hanging on the workshop wall. 'That was my first Lanc. The first crew I flew with.' There were seven airmen in the photo, three wearing peaked airman caps, two with pilot's hats and two with no hats and their hair slicked back. 'They were my mates.' He pointed to the second pilot and the Navigator. Then Grandpa waited as if gulping for air. 'I didn't like the skipper at first.' He pointed to a tall, lean man with a pilot's hat. 'Jack Dawson. Came from Western Australia, from a big station. Ran sheep. I thought he thought too much of himself. He was university educated. He didn't talk much. He stood apart from the rest of us. He'd already seen action in France.' Grandpa stopped his work on the glory box and stood in front of his black and white photograph.

'Our mission was Cologne. Night bombing. The Lanc was fully loaded with bombs. There were German searchlights looking for us. Blue lights that attached to you so that we were targets for the twin-engined Messerschmitt 110 night fighters. Hated those blue lights and the Messerschmitts. Deadly. Then there were the anti-aircraft guns. There was so much noise and smoke, planes down, bombing, fire. Jack took

our Lanc down to 2,000 feet, unloading bombs onto cities of people and falling buildings. Flak struck the Lanc, tore the guts out of the side. A shell exploded in the cockpit shattering the windscreen and the second pilot's leg, but it was Jack who got the full blast of it.' Grandpa put his heavy carpenter hands in front of his face as if to hide the image. 'A shell ripped away his right eye and the skin of his face.' It was a while before he started speaking again. 'We were screaming and firing and trying to fix the damage. Jack lost consciousness and we plummeted 800 feet before he pulled the plane out of the dive. I don't know how he did it. Even in that much pain, coughing blood, Jack had this strength. He was losing blood. A lot of blood and his face was half torn away. Bone and flesh and eyes.

Jack held that plane level, but we were low, lurching in the sky. Flak was still hitting us, but Jack held onto that plane, crossing the English Channel in the dark. We couldn't land. Not enough fuel. Too much damage. One gunner was dead. We reached the English coastline. Jack could hardly speak. 'Parachutes. Get out of here.' There was so much blood. 'An order.'

'We left Jack. Jumped. They found his body weeks afterwards, brought in with the tide on a beach.'

Grandpa was careful not to judge people too quickly after that. Grandpa told me that war is not brave, but people can be brave in war and in life.

CHAPTER 15

I wake up with a start. This is the day. I'm nervous. Jones is taking the bivvy down with military precision. The problem is that we're still under it. He must be nervous. George kept me awake on and off all night with panic breathing. He definitely is nervous. Spano kept muttering that he wants to go home. 'Shut up and go home,' we yelled at him. Spano slinks off as soon as he can. He's been tagging along with Robbo lately, which is desperate. I guess even a weed needs a mate. He'll never be mine. I can forgive most things but Spano would give up a friend to save himself. I can't forgive that.

Looks like Bennie has been kicked out of his bivvy. He's still asleep under a tree. He must have been cold. It was drizzling last night. I shudder. It means mud in the cave for sure. I wander over to Bennie. He looks frozen. The morning frost has solidified him. 'Hey, Bennie. Are you all right?' Bennie opens his eyes with this startled gaze. 'Move, Bennie. We're going.' I start knocking off ice from his sleeping bag and giving it a few pounds with my fist. 'Get up.' Bennie doesn't move. I see George carrying the dixie down to the cooking group. I call out. 'Hey, George, give me a hand.' George looks around, sees me and waves. He is wacky, that George. 'No, George come over here.' He points to himself. 'Yes, George, you. Get over here.' This concerned expression crosses his face. He drops the dixie off with the cooks, and heads towards me. 'About time, George.'

'So what's wrong?'

'Look at Bennie. Let's get him up. Those shits in his group must have thrown him out last night. Bastards. It was so bloody cold and raining.'

George looks up. 'It's not raining now.'

I roll my eyes. 'George, that's not the point.' Bennie is starting to get up. 'That's it, Bennie. Come on.' He's on his feet. We help him pack up his gear. 'Okay, you get down to breakfast and eat something, won't you?'

'It's my stomach,' he mumbles.

'So what is it? The runs?' He nods. Poor bastard. George and I head down for breakfast. Porridge and sand. It's hot and burnt. Who cares? 'George, no one cooks as good as you do.'

This smug, I-know-I'm-great smile covers his face. I laugh as I gulp down burnt porridge. Jones and I have been invited to Café Piazza Italia when we get back home, 'for the best Italian pasta', George said, 'because I'll be cooking it.' Can't wait.

Day six and we're on the morning hygiene detail. We need a volunteer garbage carrier. I have managed to escape that job so far. How do I continue to get out of it? The flies and the stink around that rotting garbage are mind blowing. Jones is our leader. He should lead by example and carry it or he can just force Spano to do it. Spano can't get help from Sarah any more. I finish breakfast quickly and race for the shovel. I'd rather do shovel duty than garbage. It's over more quickly. 'Jones I'm filling in the bog,' I tell him, then I wave the shovel around. 'Any late users? It's now or never.'

No takers. Just complaints. 'Get that shovel out of here, Knox.' 'You're bloody disgusting.' 'Shit and breakfast.' 'Maybe that's it. Shit and shit.' There's laughing.

The cooking bivvy led by Luke call out, 'You're ungrateful.' 'Dead heads.' 'Better food than you deserve.'

Insults are hurled everywhere. An empty plastic bowl is chucked at Luke, followed by lots of empty bowls and one half full one. It splatters at Spano's feet. Great shot. Should have been a little higher, that's all. I'd love to join in the porridge war, but the toilet hole calls. I leave camp with the shovel over my shoulder and head into the bush. As I get closer to it, I can smell it. I wait for a minute, stop breathing, then run to the toilet hole and shovel furiously. Then I make a dash back to a safe non-smell zone to get some more air. Another breath, another dash, more furious digging, back for air. I have to do this three times. It's covered. I'm sweating. I slam the shovel on top and pad it down. Toilet duty over.

As I head back into camp I see Spano with the garbage on his back and laugh. Jones is already leading the troops out. I join the tail end. 'Hey, Bennie, did you get your porridge?' He nods. 'Feeling better?' He shrugs. 'Look, it's only two more nights and we're home.' I don't know if Bennie even registers what I say. He has this permanent shell-shocked look on his face. Two days is a long time when you're stuck in Watts's bivvy. How do you make it with a guy like that? I would have cracked. 'Okay then, Bennie.' I move off to find Jones.

I pass the stragglers at the back, then Spano with his garbage and Robbo. It's a miserable pack. The walking is slow. Chafed legs, bruises, blisters, make it tough. It's okay for Jones who's used to a broken nose or a metal studded football kick in the shins. It's okay for me because at least I know the bush with its snakes, and no toilets. I glance back at Bennie. What does he know? He plays the trumpet for god's sake. I step up the pace to get to the front. It's getting hot, the flies have landed, and the cave hangs around us like a noose.

'Jones, hold on.' I pound towards him. The compass is in his hand. He points to a mound just ahead. 'It's over there.'

'It'll be all right, don't you think?'

'Sure.'

Seaten orders all the gear to be dumped in a pile. 'You'll only need your helmets and torches,' he says. Thump, thump, thump. No one speaks much as packs are left, torches shoved into back pockets. The dixie shines in the midday sun.

Sarah gives us a last briefing — the drop into the cave, the dark, the passages, the teamwork, the underground river. She talks for a while to Bennie, George, Spano, even Watts. It's just a quiet few words saying that we can make it. Then Seaten calls out to get moving. It isn't raining, but the soil is soggy and our boots sink into it as we climb up the mound. The long grass covers the hill and I can't see the rabbit hole entrance. Then I see it like a weeping sore. Mud.

Thick, brown, claggy mud oozes around and down the rabbit hole. I peer into it. Blackness. I move back. No one wants to go first. Luke looks around. 'I'll start.' He puts on his helmet, waves, then he's gone.

Seaten pushes Spano to the front. He's jumpy, shifting from one foot to the other. 'Get it over with.' Seaten shoves him forward. 'Jump.'

'No . . .' Spano's voice peters out.

Luke's voice blasts from below. 'Ready?'

There's elbowing, thumping from behind, as Spano is pushed closer to the hole. Spit dribbles from the corners of his mouth. He rubs the spit away with the back of his hand, but there's more spit.

'Get on with it, you bloody weed,' is slung at him from the back of the line. There is a surge forward as guys shove him towards the rabbit hole. Even though Spano is small and thin, he withstands the pressure, only shuffling slightly towards the edge. Then he can't withstand it any longer.

Spano's head flexes backwards as if for air. His mouth is cracking eggshells, crazed, open, screaming.

My stomach grips into spasms as I watch. Another down. Another. George is next. He peers into the opening that has become muddier, less distinct. I wander up to him, look in the hole. 'Spano did it.' He puts his hands around his thick neck as if to protect the oxygen he needs for survival.

'You can do it,' I tell him.

'I can't,' George whispers from dry lips, dry throat.

Watts calls out. 'What's the problem up there?' The metal tips of his boots crack twigs and soil as he presses against the line. Since Seaten has been onto him, he has had to ditch his contraband and he's edgier than ever. He's walking behind Sarah. Close. Too close. He trips onto her. I don't know what happens but Sarah jumps up kicking him hard in the calf. 'Next time it'll be higher, you jerk.' I can only half hear it. Was it an accident. Did Watts do something?

Seaten didn't see it. 'Move.' He waves George on.

George hesitates, looks at me. Then he closes his eyes and lunges into the hole, his hands still clasping his throat. He moves slowly into the mud engulfing his legs, his thighs, his belly until he stops. His hands still clinging to his throat, his elbows adhering to his chest. Too big. Too big. Stuck in mud, his feet dangle in muddy darkness, his body wedged in muddy walls, his head exposed to sun and glare. 'I'm stuck.'

'You're always stuck, George.' I bend down, breathing close to his face. 'Put your arms up. Up high.'

'I can't.' His big, red face quivers. 'I can't.'

'You can.'

The pupils of his eyes open wide, letting in too much light.

'Look at me. Are you listening? Listen.' He doesn't. I call his name. 'George, George, listen to me. Listen, I'll help you. Take your right arm and pull it up.' I lean over to him, tugging at his arm, pulling until his face is redder and the mud oozes out like gel from a tube.

Out. One arm free and reaching upwards. 'The next arm, George. The next one.' I feel breathless as if the mud is squeezing the air out of me not him. 'You can do it. You can do it by yourself. Just try, George.' George disappears.

Spano and George are now part of intestinal patterns and underground rivers. Jones is next. His muscles ripple with weight-training silver bars, rowing strong currents, tackling grass scrums. He stretches his arms exposing wiry blond hair to the sun like in a pagan ritual. No one shoves him.

'Ready,' coughs out from the hole. I'm relieved. It's George's voice. He sounds okay, or at least not panicking.

Fine perspiration wets Jones's face, burrowing into a six-day growth. Jones steps down into the black, his blondness gluing to the mud walls, squeezing sludge between fingers until he is swallowed. There is silence, then a dull thud.

Watts kicks the ground, stubbing the stones until they disintegrate under the metal tips of his boots. Watts grunts, squinting away from the glare of the sun. With hangover eyes, shot with red, he looks down the mud passageway.

'Next,' whistles disjointedly from the hole opening. Is that Jones? He sounds different.

Watts smirks over the hole. 'Arse of a hole.' He looks back at the line of remaining guys, then Sarah. 'Slut of a hole.'

'Shut up, Watts.'

'Who said that?' He looks around, bleary-eyed.

No one answers.

Seaten peers into the hole, his arms glistening in the heat. 'Ready?' he shouts down into the cavern.

'Ready,' echoes back.

It's like a funeral march. 'Next ... Next ... Next ...' Pale faces, red faces, tanned faces; trails of sweat and gas, fear and bravado.

The sliding of bodies into the hole has weakened the muddy walls, making the edges softer, the sludge a spongy plasticine. The hole is even smaller now and

I'm solid, with thick wide hands like Grandpa. Workman's hands, he'd say. I open my palms, stretching my fingers, expanding the space between each one until it hurts.

'Knox,' Seaten calls out.

Sarah is standing at the end of the line chatting. She looks at me for a moment, nods as if to say it will be all right. My stomach cramps. The hole, the dark, trapped under the ground and I am so big. I inhale a concentrated gasp, clench my fists and slide into the hole.

CHAPTER 16

I slide down the mud hole. Drop. My stomach heaves. It's dark. Not like dark night but black dark. No sunlight. I adjust my eyes. There are glimmers. I squint. A line of yellow circles flicker like glow-worms. Torches held between teeth or clasped in hands move crookedly along the wet cave floor. I look up, yelling into the hole for the next person to jump. 'Ready!' My voice travels away. I wait. There's a shout back. 'Ready!' I turn on my torch and start to crawl forwards following boots. There's mud oozing under me. I hold my head up so that I don't eat it, but mud slaps my face in regular swipes. The boots in front shove more sludge at me. I stop for a few seconds to get some distance from the boots.

I flash my torch around the passage. Limestone phalluses spear up from the ground and down from the ceiling like distorted growths. I shiver, but there isn't any room to shiver. My shoulders scrape against the walls. I creep forwards on my stomach between the crystal phalluses only stopping when those stone growths rut against me. Thoughts of Laura flash into my mind. I want to get back to her. Bloody cave.

I have photos of Laura stuck on my walls. I used the school scanner and enlarged one of her and me kissing. Sexy kissing. Mum came into my bedroom to clear out the garbage, which I hate her doing. She knows it is my space. If I want garbage there, that's what I want. Mum just comes into my room and takes the garbage. When she saw the photo of Laura and me, she asked me about her. I didn't say anything. Mum has never told me about my father. Mum has secrets. So do I. Laura is private. I just know I love her and her bellybutton ring.

When Laura went to get her bellybutton ring, I went with her. It was like having your ears pierced, she said. It wasn't true. I could tell that it hurt, but probably not as much as a nipple ring. Laura never saw my nipple rings. Laura's bellybutton ring is so sexy. She wears her jeans just under her bellybutton and her top just above.

That last time we went to the pictures I held her hand and fiddled with her bellybutton ring. The cinema was packed, so it was probably a good film, but I can't remember much of it. We made out for two hours and fifteen minutes. I worked my way up from her bellybutton ring right under her top to her breasts.

Andrew said he wanted a girl with a bellybutton ring. If you ask me, he just wants any girl. For his birthday we gave him the best present. Con and I found the perfect shop — Fetish. A plastic blow-up lady met us at the front door. Con's eyes nearly exploded when he saw the sex toys, lingerie, dog collars, and the greatest selection of porn magazines ever. Andrew would have been in heaven.

'Can I see your ID?' the man at the shop counter asked. I pulled it out with my picture plastered all over it. 'Eighteen,' he said, while I sweated. 'Okay.'

My false ID had been manufactured by the criminal element in our school. They have a great business. It cost me a night's pay at Pizza Palace. It was worth it. Con wasn't asked for his ID. He looks older.

Con and I inspected everything in Fetish seriously. It was a great two hours. This was more amazing than Andrew's Internet site. Then we found the perfect present. When I handed over twenty dollars, the shop assistant asked, 'Inflated or not?'

'Not, thanks.' I didn't want to catch the bus home with it inflated.

'You'll need a bicycle pump to get it up.'

We left Fetish with a brown paper bag. Mum wasn't home from work yet, so we were safe. Blowing it up was hilarious. The bicycle pump worked overtime. It rose like a boil. Huge and pink. Wrapping it was even more hilarious, especially when Con got stuck trying to tape the top. 'Are you desperate?' I joked. He threw the sticky tape at me hitting me on the head. 'Violence is no answer to your problem, Con. If you need to talk, just talk.'

'I'll stick this up your nose,' Con laughed.

We ended up having to wrap it in newspaper. Not enough wrapping paper. We were meeting Andrew at the cinema complex that night. Mum asked what was wrapped in the brown paper. Grandpa winked. He knew.

'Andrew's birthday. It's his present,' I mumbled. 'A foam surfboard to catch waves.'

Grandpa gave us a lift, laughing every now and then. 'Good present,' he said.

When Andrew opened the two metre penis, the entire cinema complex stopped. It was one of those great moments in life.

* * *

What? What? Some idiot has smashed his head into a stalactite. Even with his helmet on, he nearly knocked himself out. There are screams of 'crap ... bloody ... shit ... arsehole'. The bellybutton ring has gone. Andrew's giant penis has gone. There's only mud. My throat constricts and Andrew disappears. There's just the cave. I touch the dripping walls and shudder. I try to think of Laura, but can't. The walls seem to be pressing against me, wanting to bury me in slush and rock. I take deep breaths.

The passage widens. Glow-worm torches aren't in single file any more. There's a jumble of flickers. Spano has weaseled through the first part easily. I see him tagging behind Luke. He knows a safe spot. He wouldn't be next to Watts. That bastard is getting more crazy every day. I reach the group. Jones is motionless marble. 'Are you all right?' I flash my torch at him. He's sweating even though it's freezing.

'Which way?' Luke asks. Two passages lead in different directions.

No answers. George is starting to gasp. Small panting wheezes. All we need is an asthma attack here. As George looks around the panting becomes choking. He hardly made it this far and the passages look tighter than the one we've just done. 'Hey, George, help me out.' He's not listening. I grab his arm. 'Help me out of my jacket.' No response. More gasping. 'Are you useless? George, help me.' George starts to focus, mainly because I'm pinching his arm hard. 'Pull the sleeve.' George grabs onto it which is pretty tough when there's no room to stand up or move. 'Right, one arm will do.' I straighten my thermals and tighten my belt. 'Okay. Arm back in. It's bloody cold here.'

George has stopped panting. He's catching his breath. Luke waves to us that he's heading down one of the passages. He calls out, 'So who's the back-up?'

I look at Jones. He still seems frozen. No one is moving towards Luke. I crawl my way to him. 'Okay, I'm behind you.' I grab Spano's arm. 'You're coming with us.' He's small and fast. We need him.

'I can't. I hurt my hand.'

He starts to lift his hand when I slam it against the wall. 'You're bloody coming.' I shove him in front of me.

I call out, 'We're going to scout ahead.'

Luke is crawling slowly forwards. Spano is next, with me behind. The tunnel is getting narrower, the mud thicker, the stalactites more extreme. Got to keep our heads down. Luke's voice comes down the line, 'Could be another tunnel here.' He stops, waits for us to catch up. 'What do you think?' He flashes his torch down a vertical fissure. 'Could be the entrance to another passageway and the way out?'

'Okay, Spano, get down there. We'll hold your legs.'

'I can't do it.'

'Spano, give up.' I stare into his eyes, our faces nearly colliding. He's afraid. I can see it in the constricted pupils, the creases at the edge of his eyelids. But it doesn't matter that he's afraid. Everyone is afraid sometime, somewhere. 'You're going to do it.'

Luke and I barricade him in. He can't escape. Spano turns and slides towards the narrowing fissure. We hold his legs as he edges down, deeper into the fissure. We wait for Spano's call to 'let go.'

There's no call. We wait, whisper, look back, wait. Then there's the call: 'Stuck.'

'Are you sure?' I shout down the fissure.

'Stuck.'

We start to pull Spano's legs. There's a scream. 'Stuck.' Luke and I let go of Spano's legs. They don't slide down further. He is stuck. Intermittent moans tremble from the bowels of the rock. We lie there in the mud staring down at the rubber soles of Spano's boots.

'Got to get him out, Luke.'

'Got to get him out,' Luke repeats.

Don't panic. No panic. 'He got down there. He can get out.'

'How?' Luke tugs at Spano's legs again, but stops when Spano screams.

'Talk. Got to talk him out.' I clear my mind and just think of Spano. Poor bastard. It's the first time I've felt sorry for him, stuck in that black hole. 'Spano.' I call out his name. No answer. I call again. 'Spano.' There's an answer this time. A moan really. 'You know you can get out of there. You got in, didn't you?'

'Can't.'

'You got in, didn't you?' I repeat the question until Spano is concentrating on the answer, until he says yes.

'You can get out.'

There's silence. That's good. At least he's not fighting me. He's got to come with me on this one . . . trust me. 'You can get out.' I say it like I believe it. I do believe it, otherwise he won't. 'Just wriggle a bit.' I wait. 'Are you wriggling?'

'A bit.' 'Bit.' 'Bit,' jabbers out of the dark.

'Great.' I can't believe he's doing what I ask. 'Wriggle some more. Are you doing it?'

'Yes.'

'See. There's room. You can feel the space. Can you feel it?'

'Okay.'

'Push your arms against the walls and shuffle. Are you doing that?' I wait. 'Shuffle.'

'Shuffle,' grunts back at me.

'Okay, then. We're going to grab your feet now. Can you feel us doing that?'

'Sure.'

'When you've got your space right and your arms are shoving against the wall, we'll pull. We'll just wait until you're ready. You give the shout. Okay?'

We wait for Spano. It's long, like waiting desperately for a pardon before an execution. It's forever. Luke wants to try and pull him up now. I shake my head. 'He's got to make the call himself. Otherwise it won't work.' Luke argues a bit, but backs off.

Then there's a call. 'Ready.'

'Ready,' I shout down and Luke and I pull. The buckle of Spano's boots digs into my hand. We pull. Luke is using all his force. Spano is screaming. There's a give, a lever. We drag ourselves back and Spano is being dragged up and back too. Out. Out.

Spano has red scratches down the side of his face. I collapse burrowing my face in my arms. 'Shit, Spano.' I want to be sick. We lie in the mud panting. 'Shit, Spano, shit.'

We crawl slowly back to the rest of them waiting. 'What took you so long?' There's this nervous smell of sweat and farts. 'Thought you weren't coming back.'

'Funny,' I throw back at them. 'Wrong passage. It's that way.'

Luke leads and I hang back slotting into the middle with Spano. We crawl next to each other as the passage has widened again. No one talks much. We grovel on our stomachs, grunting, watching our heads. Bennie moves like a snail, trailing at the back. He doesn't talk any more, keeps himself separate. He's still got the runs and has to stop every now and then. He stinks. We seem to be moving upwards. A shout echoes down the line: 'Cave, cave.' We crawl towards it. There's a stench, a rancid, murky smell. There's space to crawl on your knees now. The opening is small, but the ceiling is higher. There's a cavern to the left. A pitch black stinking tunnel. Torches flash into it and there are screams as bats dive and perch and we're crawling so fast, we don't care that we're eating mud and ripping legs. We're moving, moving downwards. Sliding like shit down into wetter, muddier passages.

CHAPTER 17

'Need a piss,' George whispers in my ear.

'Hold on.' I keep crawling forwards trying to keep my head low enough not to crash into the ceiling and high enough not to swallow mud. I hate this mud. Where is that bloody river?

George shakes his head. 'Can't hold on.'

'What?' My knees are raw.

'Need a piss.'

Who cares? 'Piss your pants, then.' When will we get there?

'*You* piss your pants if you want.'

'I don't have to go.' I flash my torch at him. His face is screwed up damming back an ocean. 'Go to the back of the line. Do it there.' I crawl on. Idiot George had to have that bottle of water before we dropped down here. What's he want me to do? Piss for him? I crawl up to Jones. 'George needs a piss.' Jones doesn't look at me. He's got some sort of tremor. 'Are you all right?' I flash my torch at him. His eyes register nothing. They are pinpoints of blue, like ice specks. 'It's me. Knox.'

He whispers: 'I've got to get out of here.'

'We'll be out soon.'

'Can't take it.' The shaking is barely controlled. 'I can't breathe in here.' His face is crazing like shattered glass.

'It's okay. We're nearly at the river.'

'I've got to get out.' Suddenly he is kicking the walls and thumping the limestone with his torch.

'Calm down, Jones,' but he doesn't calm down. The marble is splitting into fragments.

'Let me out.'

'We'll be out soon, Jones.' He can't hear me. He is breathing too fast, panting, flooding himself with oxygen. I try to grab his arms, but he belts me with the back of his hand. I reel backwards.

The sweat is pouring off him. His Viking face is exploding. 'Get out of my bloody way. Stuff off, you bastards.'

My face is throbbing as I crawl back towards him, but not too close. 'Shit, Jones. Stop. You can't get out this way. There's a bloody mountain above us. Stop.' He can't hear me and keeps bashing, trying to kick his way through it.

No one can get near him. Luke tries and gets a kick in his guts. Spano moves away to safety. Jones's boots can break someone's jaw if they make contact. He's smashing the guts out of himself against the wall and he'll smash anyone in his way. We've got to grab his feet and arms so that we can drag him to the river. The tunnel is tight and Jones is too big and strong. I point to Luke. 'You get his left leg. I'll take his right.' George has scrambled up from the back. 'You get his right arm, George.'

Watts crawls towards Jones. His eyes are feral. A shiver creeps down my neck. Watts looks at me, then says, 'I'll take his left arm.'

Watts. This feels wrong. Why would Watts want to help Jones? Everyone has stopped moving. The noise of Jones's shouting crashes against the underground walls, echoing and re-echoing in machine gun barrages. Jones is spitting saliva. A great caged white bear — growling teeth, dangerous attacks, trapped defences.

Luke hovers, ready to move. 'What are we waiting for, Knox?' I stare at Watts again, hesitate. Luke yells at me, 'There's enough of us. Let's move.'

I look at Watts, then Jones.

'Do you want to watch Jones kill himself?'

'No. All right then.' I nod. 'When I say go, we jump him.' George leans forward ready. Luke leans forward. I lean forward. Watts leans. Adrenaline. 'Wait, wait. Ready? We'll jump him together.' I shout out. 'Go.'

We charge Jones. George flattens his right arm. Sumo is lying on it like a whale. Luke has his left leg. I have the right. Jones is thrashing around pinned to the floor by three of us when Watts's army boots crack against his spine. Jones gasps, spit dribbling out of his mouth like blood.

'You arsehole.' I kick at Watts. 'You bastard.' His fists go for me. I let go Jones's arm. Watts just misses my eye, punching my cheek. Pain sears through my face and I pound at him in the dark, hitting rock, crushing my hand. Watts goes for me again. Everyone is shouting. Arms and legs all over the place. Watts is stronger than I am. He's got me in a headlock. I blearily see his face, when his grip starts to loosen. I try to focus. What's happening? Squinting, I see Bennie. He is lying on Watts, thumping his fists into his back, again and again. Other guys jump on, thumping that arsehole. Then he's down. Out.

I lie there on my back, exhausted. Sucking my knuckles, I taste blood. The coldness of rock and the oozing of mud slowly penetrates my body, anaesthetising the pain of smashed arms and grazed legs. The noise of the fight has disappeared into echoes that are dying into whispers. Watts is down like a Messerschmitt. Crashed with no army to support him.

I'm so tired. I don't know what this is about. Why am I here? I vaguely see someone crawling forward. 'Bennie?' I whisper, fighting for breath.

Bennie bends over me with crinkling eyes. 'Are you okay?'

I nod. 'Thanks, Bennie.'

I can't move, but I don't want to stay buried in this tomb for the rest of my life. Gradually, I roll onto my stomach and get back onto my knees. The line starts crawling towards the river. Jones is being dragged down the passageway by Luke and George. Watts has been left lying on the ground. Guys move around him, leaving Watts sprawled in the mud. No one acknowledges him. They just keep moving. Watts broke the code. He went for Jones when Jones was down.

Each drag forward is fighting glue. Drag, pull, shuffle. I look up. There's light. Luke is standing. George is standing. Torches flood the opening as more and more of us land. The cave opens into a chamber. Torches flash to limestone formations, ledges, cracks and fissures. It's not a large space, but there is room to bend, stretch, stand. Standing. Luxury. My knees feel like shit. I look like shit. Everyone does. Mud ferals.

Jones is sitting with his head bent into his hands. There's no panic on his face any more, but he looks shell-shocked. George is sitting next to him.

Luke yells out, 'River.' The word passes along. Torches focus on the hollow. The pool of black water. There is an eerie silence. We're here. I crouch at the edge. I can't see how deep it is or what lies under the water. I put my hand into it. Freezing. Others follow. 'Freezing.' 'Freezing.' 'Freezing.'

Luke stands at the edge. 'I'm going down to have a look.' He concentrates on the pool for a few minutes. Takes a breath. Jumps. There's silence as he submerges. We wait. Long seconds. There's a splash. Luke's head bobs up like a cork. 'Bloody icy. Hard to breathe down there.' His face is pale. His lips are blue. 'Jump. Touch the wall. Follow it. It's at the bottom of the wall. The hole. Get through it. Okay.' There are questions but Luke has submerged again and he's gone.

There's talk. 'The hole.' 'How far?' 'Nearly out.' Spano whispers, 'I've heard someone got stuck in that hole under the water. Drowned. I heard that.'

'Shut up, Spano.' I shove him into the pool. He's gone.

I've got to get Jones. He's slouched against a limestone column by himself. I crouch beside him. 'Peter, we're here.' He doesn't move. 'You have to dive under that wall and then you're out of here.'

Jones still doesn't move.

'Are you ready?' I wait.

I shiver when I see Jones's Viking face. It seems to be etched with cracks. 'Ready?' The cracks harden with his words. 'Out of here.' The icy spark is in his eyes again.

I want to speak to him. Not now, but some day. If he can. 'I'll jump in with you.'

'No.' Then he does something strange. A man's thing to do. He shakes my hand. His grip is strong. 'I broke down, didn't I?'

I look into the pool. I nod.

'Thanks.' Jones looks like he wants to say something else. He doesn't. He closes down. Talk, Jones, talk. No. He stares at me for a moment but there's an expression that is different. Talking. It's simple, but it's not. It was easier when Grandpa and I talked. The world made more sense. Grandpa. A wave of heat floods my body. After he died, I stopped talking to Mum. I couldn't any more. Suddenly, my mind stumbles. It's like hanging from the rope on the chimney.

Jones stands up. He's unsteady. He finds George. Shakes his hand, then walks to the black ice water. His eyes focus on the pool. There are murmurs from guys waiting their turn. He takes off his helmet and puts it under his arm. Then Jones jumps, disappearing into blackness.

I wait at the edge, flash my torch at the black water. Acid rises into my throat. What if I can't find the escape hole? What if I get stuck like Spano said? What if I find Jones's body wedged in the hole? I turn off my torch and yell, 'I'm going.' I take a huge breath and plunge into icy water. The cold is like shock. I want to let go of my air, but don't. I reach for the wall, struggle down it. The opening. Can't breathe, can't see. Must be it. I'm suffocating. Get through it. Can't. Push. Slide. Through it. Up, up. Light. Sunlight.

I let out an enormous breath. Gasp for air. Turning my face to the sky I feel the sun, see the blue. Relief. I yell out, 'Yahoo.' There are 'yahoos' back. Then I dive in and out of the water. Wild diving. It's cold, freezing cold, but after the underground icy cave water it feels warm. And there's no mud. No clinging, sticky, filthy mud. I dive and dive. Luke is splashing. George is rolling like a hippo. Bennie is jumping.

We're out of the cave.

CHAPTER 18

Post-cave euphoria is gone. There's just exhaustion. Tiredness like lead. Duties completed. Tents, toilet, hygiene, fire, food. The camp ready for night.

Seaten is fired with enthusiasm racing between bivvies and duties. 'You all did it.' It's like his personal achievement.

Sarah is quieter about it. 'Was it all right?' she asks me.

I don't know. 'I did it.' I wander off to collect more firewood. I want to get away from her and everyone. Was it all right? I know that I can squeeze into mud holes and climb in darkness and be smashed and dive into fear. Did I know that before? I collect small branches and pile them in a store next to a huge ghost gum with peeling bark and a white underbelly. I press my head against the white underbelly.

Did I know that before? 'Yes.' I say it aloud so that I can hear it. 'Yes.' I put my hands in front of my face and let the sobs from deep inside me vomit to the surface. 'Yes, I knew.'

You fight when you have to. You try to survive when you have to. You're brave when you have to be.

I don't understand why we went into the cave. Why we are on this trek to nowhere, for no one? There is no war here. I don't want war. I've seen Grandpa's friends. I hid behind Grandpa when I first saw the Navigator with his scarred face. His burnt arms and legs and back. The burns on his face made a monster. Grandpa's leg had been shattered by shrapnel, but he went back for the Navigator. Pulled him out of fire and flames. Grandpa saved the Navigator. Four crewmen died. They gave Grandpa the Distinguished War Medal for bravery.

When I got older, I was ashamed that I'd ever hid from the Navigator because of his face. Later I didn't see the scars. The Navigator came camping with us sometimes. He was a good fisherman.

What is the point of this camp? To hate the bush because the struggle has taken away the beauty? To walk and only see our feet and the dirt underneath them? To carry Spano's backpack? To fight against Watts and his aggression? I clench my teeth. To see Jones break? Seaten thinks there's a reason to be here. I look at my cut hands. Seaten doesn't even know who I am. How can he know what this camp will mean to me? He doesn't know that my grandfather died and left us reeling like fish on a line. Suddenly everything begins to swirl around me and waves of nausea start me heaving. I reach for my mouth trying to pull out the hook. But it rips, rips. I am afraid that I'll be alone.

I slide against the trunk of the ghost gum sitting on bark and dirt. Taking deep breaths, I close my eyes. Since the funeral, thoughts of my father have drifted inside my head. I asked Grandpa once about him.

He'd rubbed his chin for a while, then said, 'Sam, if you need to find him, I'll help you.' It would cut my mother's heart out if I did. I hate Mum for that.

The camp is quiet. We eat our meal. Our breaths blow white puffs into the cold night air. Scrogan is passed around. George takes the chocolate bits. Sarah congratulates us on our achievement. I can't look at her when she says that. Jones screaming like a trapped animal, Watts's boots, George pissing underground.

Seaten comes over to me. 'Jones doesn't want to navigate. Last day tomorrow,' he says. 'You can lead that one.' He talks to me differently these days.

I wander over to Jones and slump beside him. 'We have got to get over there.' I point to the map.

Jones shrugs.

'What do you think of going around the base of the mountain? It's flat and we're all too tired to climb.'

Jones stares at the food in his plastic bowl.

'Peter. I need you for this.'

'You don't.'

'I do.' I flatten the map out in front of him. 'It's too much by myself. You know what these guys are like? They'll kill me if I go the wrong way.' I wait. 'You've been doing it for the whole expedition. Are you sick of it?'

'Maybe.'

'Come on, Peter. We need your mapping.' I hesitate. 'And you.'

His face creases into doubt. 'All right.' We work out the flattest route possible, even if it is longer. We find a creek for our lunch stop and where to abseil on our final descent into camp. These are tired guys.

'Tomorrow night, we meet up with the other group.' I fold the map. 'Andrew and Con are in that group. You know them.'

Jones nods. They aren't his friends.

Jones and I head off to our bivvy. Need sleep. I wave at Bennie who's dragging his sleeping bag to a place far away from Watts's bivvy. Watts is ready to kill him since the cave. George is already snoring with his beanie pulled over his face, his boots on and his arms inside his sleeping bag. The dixie is shiny, sitting like a trophy outside the tent. I snarl at Spano. Nothing has changed. Well, it has. I never liked him, but now I realise there are some worms that slide through the earth pouring out shit, without turning the soil. He's a waste of space. I think of him stuck in the crevasse. Maybe not. I don't know.

Jones slots into his sleeping bag. He doesn't look at me. It's like he can't. I want to tell him that he's still the leader. Not the only leader, but a leader. I lie there next to him listening to his breathing. 'Jones.' His eyes blink open. 'The cave was tough.' I hesitate. 'Everyone felt trapped down there. But we all survived it.'

He turns his head towards me. 'I didn't.'

I want to argue, but can't cut through the marble. 'Can you live with what happened down there?'

'No.' He speaks slowly. 'I never thought I'd break.' He blinks hard. 'I feel like a coward.'

'Coward? Peter, you will never be a coward.' I wait. 'But you're human, like the rest of us.'

And the rain comes. It pours in buckets and the dirt turns to mud and the mud rivers around and between us. The dixie overflows making a waterfall into our bivvy. George turns it upside down. We huddle closer to each other. Sleeping bag against sleeping bag and I try to dream of Laura and home. Then the hail comes. Pelting ice-bullets tearing the tent, machine gunning the bivvies, and freezing exposed noses into icicles. I pull my beanie over my nose.

In the morning it stops. Just like that. No hail, no rain. Just the sun, rising yellow in grey skies. I laugh. Last day today. Last day.

Soggy bodies pack up soggy tents. We squelch past each other to eat our soggy breakfast in front of a fire that doesn't warm because it's too wet. There's smouldering, dirty smoke and Seaten organising more wood. Sarah shakes her head at Seaten.

No one even whinges. We can smell home. Everyone wants to get moving. There'll be leeches for sure. I stretch my stiff joints, bandage my hands and sling my pack on my shoulders. We look to Jones. He's standing unsure at the start of a new day. Luke paces up to him. 'Are we going?' he asks expectantly.

Jones looks at him strangely. Then he waves the trek forwards. 'We're heading this way.' Jones leads us out.

Wet clothes are cold and chafe between our legs. I keep looking up at the sun, willing it to rise further and beat down on us and dry our clothes. They'll be dry by the afternoon. I move towards the back of the line. Bennie is trailing behind everyone else. He must have had a rotten night. At least the runs aren't so bad for him since he's stopped eating. He still smells of shit all the time. 'How is it going?' He holds his stomach. The yellowness of his face is like a ghoul, with hollow eyes.

Bennie grimaces. 'Watts doesn't appreciate the trumpet much.'

A joke? I smile. I don't know how Bennie can joke when he looks like this. 'That bastard doesn't appreciate much. It'd be great to see a trumpet stuffed up his arse.'

Bennie smiles.

'Thanks for helping me in the cave.'

'It's okay.' Bennie stumbles over the words. 'I did it for me as well as you.'

Bennie and I walk slowly together at the back of the pack. 'Well, I'm grateful.'

He whispers with a surprised look on his face: 'I didn't know I could hate.' Bennie bends over cramping, then rushes for the bushes.

The heat is rising, as is the humidity that makes us clammy wet. I don't know what is worse, cold wet or humid wet. The battalions of bush flies arrive. They've missed us and dive for sweaty foreheads and dripping necks. Their headquarters are on Luke's back. The rotting garbage is mountainous now. I avoid him and catch up with Jones. We look at the map as we trek forwards.

The track is mucky with pools of rainwater waiting for the sun to suck them up. The leeches will be enjoying themselves. I shudder but I don't care. They can suck my blood today. Tomorrow is home. There'll be mosquitoes but I don't care. They can suck my blood today. Tomorrow is home.

Home. I wonder what Mum is doing. I promised Mum that I'd go with her to see Grandpa's grave. His ashes were dug into Grandma's grave. He'd be happy being there with her. That's where I want to be buried one day. Mum asked me to visit the grave with her. I made excuses. Mum thinks I don't care. I do, I do.

I just couldn't see Grandpa's ashes then. It would mean that he was really dead. Really gone. It would mean that I have to think about the Navigator's last words to me.

'I don't know if you'll understand this now, but I want to tell you now.' He spoke slowly, definitely. 'Your grandfather was my friend in war and after.' He coughed, gulping down air as if catching his breath. 'Your grandfather lead without wanting leadership. He taught by example. He was there for his family and friends but he had flaws like all of us. He didn't let your mother grow her own wings, fly by herself, and she'll find life hard without him. He refused to be part of what he didn't believe in even though he could have made a difference. But he made a difference to us. He loved the bush, his carpentry, helping you become a man.'

He looked me in the eyes, forcing me to look back. 'Even though he's gone, he'll always be a part of you. I know you'll find it hard. But you have to take what he gave you and grow from it.'

I hear the Navigator now.

CHAPTER 19

Watts hauls Robbo over into the bush. I don't know what Watts does to Robbo, but he is on Watts's team again. I look to the back of the line and see Bennie struggling. Poor Bennie. But he did stand up to Watts. Bennie, who is in hiding most of the time or strategically placing himself next to Sarah or Seaten. Bennie, who has no friends on this camp. He didn't kowtow to Watts. He'll sleep in hail, on rocks, with his guts cramping blood, but that trumpet player didn't give in to Watts. I want to hear him play that trumpet. Maybe I'll get Andrew and Con to come with me and listen to his band.

Sarah catches up with me. She wants to talk about organising the packing. 'Everything has to be accounted for. Can you check that everyone has got the camping gear in your bivvy group?'

I hold up the nail brushes. 'And we haven't lost the dixie.'

She laughs. 'George and that dixie. I think they'll miss each other after the camp.' She looks across at George. 'I was worried when I first saw George. Thought he'd have trouble on the trek.'

'He did.' I pause. 'But he's a good guy.'

'That's what this camp is about. Finding out that George is a good guy.'

I shake my head. 'It's a tough way to find out.'

She says that testing yourself makes you feel that you can achieve anything. 'Can you believe you did this trek? You got through the cave?' I listen. Her eyes light up and I know she's a believer. I like Sarah. I like the way her hair bobs and the way her thermals stick out of her shorts. When she swam that freezing river, she was amazing. I like the way she helped Bennie or crouched beside me overlooking the valleys. But can't she see? There are other ways to find out that George is a good guy. I don't understand this way. I didn't want to see Jones in the cave. I didn't want to see the bush as my enemy. I didn't want to feel hate.

'Didn't you discover some things about yourself that you never knew before?'

I shrug.

'I saw qualities in you which I didn't know were there in the beginning.'

I laugh. 'What qualities?'

She smiles. 'You think about that yourself.'

The trekking is hypnotic. One boot in front of the other, squashing sludge, clambering over fallen trees. There will be plenty of mud in the cave. Hope Andrew and Con survive it. No one talks. Sarah walks beside George, pacing him so that he doesn't fall behind. Luke is matching Jones's strides at the front. Seaten is stomping beside me. His hair is flecked with mud. His face is sunburnt. I stare at him. I don't like Seaten. His mind is like a box. Open. Shut. Black. White. Rigid with no in-betweens. I have something I need to tell him: not that my feet are blistered and aching; not that my grandfather died; not that the cave is obscene. But if I tell him, the box will be open. I won't be able to close it. I keep in step with Seaten. He turns to look at me and increases his pace. So do I.

'Do you want something, Knox?'

'Yes.'

Seaten raises his eyebrows curious. 'All right.'

'It's Watts.'

Seaten nods. 'I know about him.'

'Not this. You don't know this.'

Seaten stops increasing his pace. We walk side by side silently. 'Watts.' Suddenly I feel the fear of his fists, his threats. Watts could get me for this, but I can't leave it any more. I want to beg Seaten to keep this a secret: beg him not to tell anyone that I'm the snitch. I'm scared that when Watts finds out, he'll pin me against the toilet wall and bash the shit out of me. But I can't hide. If I tell, Watts will know. I look back. Watts has already regrouped. There are three of them. I look ahead and see Luke and Jones. George is carrying his Dixie on his back. 'Watts.' It's the Rave. It's Annie who was too scared to tell because no one would stand beside her. The Rave. My stomach churns. Just spit it out, Knox. Spit it out. I jerk the words. 'Watts raped a girl. In the urinal. At the last Rave.'

Seaten's face seems to match his red hair. 'Rape?' His face creases into sunburnt lines across his forehead. Seaten wants details. I stare at him dazed. I can't give him details now. I've told, re-opened a night no one wants to remember. Isn't that enough for now?

No. Seaten questions and I understand why I dislike him. I try to escape, walking faster and faster. Seaten keeps up with me and the questions keep coming. I answer, but he keeps asking for more. Shut up, Seaten. Shut up. I can't answer. My legs are rubber, my mind is exploding. My answers deteriorate into monosyllables.

Seaten puts his hand on my shoulder. He's never done that before. 'It's okay, Knox. We'll do the rest later.' He flicks a look at Watts. There's disgust in his eyes. Then he looks at me. It's different. Would Seaten have believed me before? He believes me. It feels like respect.

I trek faster. Lunch is quick. Everyone is keen to move on, like wild horses sensing home territory. There is the climb now. Not too high, but rugged on grazed knees and torn muscles. Two hours in the blazing heat. Sweat drips off my face. I can't think. Don't want to. I just want to climb. Then there's the top, with the view out over valleys and riverbeds. I scream as I abseil off the peak feeling the wind swish against me and the rush of speed and flying. I scream.

Last campsite. Last campsite. I've been waiting for so long. I'm desperate to see Andrew and Con. Group A straggle into camp, dirty and exhausted. The instructors shake hands and start their postmortem. Group A didn't make the cave. The news spreads like wildfire. I shake my head. I don't know what that means. Seaten is exploding with pride.

I shake my head. The cave. We made it. So does that make us heroes and them cowards? Or does it mean they have the courage to say no and we are the sheep that will follow orders into hell? There was no point to the cave. I'm just glad we're all back. I see Andrew. He's as filthy as we are. He sticks his finger up at me. I smile. It's great to see that rude finger. Con stares at the ground. There is no contact between the groups. No talk. Too soon. Private, taboo. We stay in our groups. The comfort of routine sets in. Tents up, toilet, hygiene, fire, cooking.

Dinner is massive. The left-over provisions of the week are all piled in the dixie — flour and beans and spam. Chilli sauce and soy and salt and pepper. The dixie is overflowing and George is in charge. It feels good to see George ladling out our last dinner. Group A and Group B sit apart. I look over at Andrew stuffing his face. Con isn't eating much. His eyes are ringed with black circles. It's good to see them, but we don't talk. Can't.

Our final night sleeping on rocks, under plastic. I check the ropes to make sure they're tight. Last night, Luke's bivvy crashed down under the force of the hail. The ropes had split. I check the knot tying our bivvy to a tree. It's all fine, when I hear a croak. Another one. I look around. A lime green tree frog is singing to me. Where did he come from? In all this mud and slush, there he is. Clean, green and beautiful. I start to laugh. His cartoon face smiles at me with a big froggy grin. 'Come here, little frog.' I pick him up. He squats on the palm of my hand. The pads of his feet are soft. George hovers over to me and pats him. Then I put him back on his branch and he sings again. Maybe he knows we're going home.

It hurts to roll over. It hurts to move. George slots into his position. I slide beside him. Next, there is Spano. Then Jones. 'Home tomorrow.' It feels good saying it aloud. It makes tomorrow closer. Spano is shaking. I squint at him as he gulps back sobs. He burrows into his sleeping bag and his sobs become muffled so that no one hears. Sleep. Rocks jut into my back. I shift. I hear voices, campfire movements, the small green frog croaking, Seaten's voice. I close my eyes. I don't know if I should have told Seaten about the Rave.

The Rave was alcohol free except for the flasks hidden in back pockets and the stash planted in the garden beds. I'd had two shots of vodka at Andrew's before we came. He stole it from his brother's bar fridge. There was plenty of cheap Ecstasy at the Rave. Some of the guys at school were suppliers. Made a bit of profit and could get their stuff for free. Forty dollars a go. Then all-night dancing and delirium. I didn't bring money. Good excuse not to buy and no one would give you any for nothing. I don't do Ecstasy. Andrew doesn't either. Alcohol and girls are Andrew's speed, except for his one-off magic mushroom trip.

I didn't want to be out of my brain. Didn't want to get up the next morning stoned when I was working at Pizza Palace that day. When Laura might come in and order a ham and pineapple pizza.

After the toilet window and the broken ladder, after the stinking alleyway, I groped back inside and stood leaning against the wall. Sweaty dancing, techno music, guys falling out of the toilets. Watts came out of the urinals pumping his balls. Robbo laughed. I shoved my way through the moshing to look for Andrew. Found him.

'Piss off,' he elbowed me. Andrew was making out with a 'hot chick' according to him.

'Come on, Andrew.'

'I'm coming on, all right.' He laughed. 'Get your own chick.'

Andrew was out of it. 'You're coming with me.' I dragged him behind me and he dragged the chick, until she got caught up in the mosh and he lost her.

'You bastard, Knox.'

'Shut up, Andrew.'

One guy was vomiting down the side of one urinal. The other urinals were empty. Annie was on the floor leaning over her knees. Her pants were ripped and lying on the caramel ceramic tiles. 'Annie . . .' I bent down next to her. 'Annie.' She didn't look up. I could see red thumbprints on her pale arms. 'Can you get up?'

'No,' she whispered.

I didn't ask her what happened. Andrew didn't ask. We helped her stand, but she crumpled back onto the floor. Her top was torn. A red line marked her left breast like a can had been scrapped across it. I took off my jacket and put it around her. We helped her walk out of there through to the alleyway.

Andrew said it was up to Annie to tell. She was too scared. I said we should tell. We waited for something to happen. Nothing did and Andrew forgot it. I didn't.

The Rave goes in and out of my thoughts. I can't sleep. I doze. Hear the green frog. Wake. Think. Wait for the morning.

CHAPTER 20

Morning. Day eight. I wake up with a start. I must have finally got to sleep. Rubbing my eyes, I search for the frog on the branch. Gone. I brush the frost from my sleeping bag. I look at us, huddled green sausages next to each other. Four peas in a pod. I nudge George. 'We made it, Sumo. Sumo the Great.'

George's face breaks into a great smile. 'Yes, we did.'

Jones stands to stretch. He looks more like a Viking than ever with his blond hair and blond curling beard.

'You should keep that look,' I say. 'Viking Jones.'

'If only I was.' Jones runs his fingers through the knots in his hair.

Spano crawls out of his pod. 'We'll be home today, Spano.' I see the redness in his eyes and actually feel sorry for him. I don't hate him today. I don't have to. Camp is over. Spano is out of my life. He'll never be in it again.

Packing up is intense. Everything is stuffed into backpacks. No need now for easy access to torches, sunscreen, mosquito repellent, hats. Nothing left out, except the filthy clothes we are standing in. Bivvies are pulled down. Tent site is cleared. Garbage is carried to the campfire. Plastics dumped in the garbage bins to be taken to the tip. The last toilet hole is covered. The disinfectant bowl emptied. Luke is pretty funny when he returns the shit-hole spade to Seaten. He wraps the handle in a toilet paper ribbon (unused) and crowns Seaten with a roll of cardboard from the middle of a toilet roll. Everyone cheers and Seaten actually laughs and makes a royal bow. Then it is back to serious organisation. 'Water bottles over here.' He counts and recounts. 'Bottles missing.' Orders are belted out in all directions. 'Pile all the gear that belongs to the expedition over there.' He points to each bivvy group. 'The expedition truck will collect this later.'

Sarah is making a checklist. Bivvy ropes. Missing. Karabiners. Missing. Small frying pan. Missing. Iodine bottle. Spano produces it. 'Here,' he calls out. George shouts. 'I've got the dixie.' Everyone laughs.

There is so much missing. 'You have to pay for it,' Sarah says. 'I'm not interested in who lost it, destroyed it or ate it. It's going to be divided up between you equally and you all have to pay.' I can see I'll have to do a few extra shifts at Pizza Palace. Who cares, we're out of here.

I walk beside Bennie to our last breakfast. 'I'm looking forward to getting out of here.'

'Yes.' Bennie squints at Watts who is already at breakfast.

I have to ask him. He did save me from Watts. At least I have to know. 'Bennie, what's your name?'

He looks at me strangely. 'Bennie.'

'No. Your first name.' I hesitate. 'I'd like to know it.' I hesitate again. 'Because you're a mate.'

Bennie waits for a while. 'Okay then. Simon.'

The groups join up. There are waves, nods. I punch Andrew in the arm. He punches me back. No one eats much. Too much anticipation. We're stopping for hamburgers at lunchtime. There are big plans to eat the hamburger joint out of all their burgers and drink all their milkshakes. Breakfast packed up. Fire stamped out. 'Let's go.' Jones doesn't have to lead. There are no stragglers. Backpacks on. We follow the instructors. The track is a marked dirt path. An easy half-hour walk. Then we see it, like a mirage. The buses. Civilisation.

Sarah calls our group over. Seaten stands next to her. 'It was a great expedition. There were some funny times. Some serious. You'll remember this. I know I will. It's been great. Have a good trip home.'

Luke calls out a cheer. Everyone follows. Three times.

We hear Andrew's and Con's group cheer their instructor. I glance over and see an assassin-lookalike. I'm glad we had Sarah. She walks over to me before I board the bus. 'Have you discovered your qualities yet?'

I crinkle my eyes half shut. 'Not really.'

'By the end of this expedition, everyone except a few like Watts, looked to you for leadership. Think about that.' She is serious. 'It's a great thing.'

We board our buses. Watts and his group sit at the back. They're ignored. There are jokes about digging a toilet at the back of the bus. Then there are others.

'What about sand? We need it for our hamburgers.'

'And where are the rocks? How can we sleep on these seats without them?'

'I brought back a friendly snake.' Luke throws his belt down the aisle to shouting voices. 'Kill the snake. Kill the snake.'

'Keep it down,' Seaten blasts back.

The jokes keep coming fast and thick until everyone is settled into their seats. I'm next to George. Andrew sticks his thumb up at me as his bus pulls away. Con waves. We'll catch up on the weekend. The jokes stop. Sarah is standing outside the bus with her feet apart in her dirty thermals with tennis ball tits. She's waving as the bus moves down the road.

The talking quietens to whispers. Then the bus is quiet. Day eight. We'll be home soon. Snoring, grunting, sleeping. I close my eyes. Annie. Watts. I try to block him out, but he knifes his way into my mind. No, I don't want to think of him now. No, go away. Tomorrow. Watts is for tomorrow. My heart is thudding and I open my eyes to see George snoring. A smile crosses his face. I watch him for a while, relieved. George.

Slowly, my eyes close again as Watts disappears and I imagine an eagle gliding over valleys. The next camping trip will be with Andrew and Con. It will be different to this. Then there's Laura. She'll be waiting for my phone call. I'll ring her tonight.

I open my eyes, glance out of the window. Mum will be waiting to collect me when the coach pulls into the school grounds. I whistle a relieved sigh. Mum will have left work early, have dinner ready in the oven, put out clean towels and run a hot bath. I want to talk to Mum, tell her that we can go to Grandpa's grave. Maybe I'll ask her about my father. I don't know. I feel exhaustion descending to sleep. I'm going to visit the Navigator. Then I'm dreaming that I'm in Grandpa's workshop finishing the glory box, hammering with Grandpa's hammer, sanding with Grandpa's sander, looking out of the workshop window at lorikeets splashing in the birdbath Grandpa made for them.

About the Author

You'll find Gervay planting 3000 mangroves in Kiribati as part of a mission for action against climate change. In Istanbul speaking to 1000s of young people about NO bullying. In remote Aboriginal communities supporting education. In a juvenile detention centre sharing books with teenage girls. At the World Burn Congress in New York presenting 'how the inner person can triumph over a preoccupation with surface scars and know that basic values of commitment, caring and trust are more important than the texture of the skin. Butterflies is a stunning insight. ' Dr Hugh Martin, President of the Australian and New Zealand Burn Association and Head of the Burn Unit, The Children's Hospital Sydney

Why? Gervay's passion is empowering people to be critical thinkers and develop the resilience to advocate for justice. As the child of refugees, growing up with the emotional complexities of parents who had been through the Holocaust, migration and loss, books were Gervay's source of escape, comfort, insight and courage.

Gervay tackles themes from feminism in *Shadows of Olive Trees*, harmony and inclusion in *Elephants Have Wings*, extremism and war in *Heroes of the Secret Underground*, consent and control in *The Edge of Limits*. What she writes matters to her deeply and is grounded in personal experience.

Gervay has been awarded the Lifetime Social Justice Literature Award by the International Literacy Association, Order of Australia, nominee for Australia for Astrid Lindgren Memorial Award, among other awards. Her acclaimed stories are published in prestigious literary journals and anthologies including the Indian-Australian anthologies alongside the works of Sir Salman Rushdie and Thomas Keneally. She represented Australia in 'Peace Story' an IBBY, UNICEF anthology with 22 authors, 22 illustrators from 22 countries. She continues to write for pathways to peace.

Her books are endorsed by The Cancer Council, Room to Read, Books in Homes reaching Indigenous and disadvantaged children, Life Education, many anti bullying and literacy organisations. Susanne heads the Society of Children's Book Writers & Illustrators (ANZ), is patron of Monkey Baa Theatre, ambassador for Room to Read, Reading and literacy Ambassador for many campaigns and is an acclaimed national and international speaker.

sgervay.com

It's the time of the emerging women's movement. It's the 70's. Sexuality, love, passions, creativity, the dynamic changes of the second rise of feminism. There's a new world of freedom for young women. Tessa is on her beginning feminist journey, torn between the traditions of her Greek family and the independence of a changing world of equal rights. There are her friends, Athena who is second generation Greek and Jenny who is sixth generation British. There's love. Even a handsome Mr Darcy. There's literature. Threats of an arranged marriage. The pill. The first women's refuge. Coercive control. The pull of religion and ethics that challenge women's rights.

'A story of women's empowerment set against a background of the emerging women's movement, *Shadows of Olive Trees* has relevance today. Reminding me of Looking for Alibrandi. Gervay gets better with every book' *Spectrum, Sydney Morning Herald*

sgervay.com/shadows-of-olive-trees
ISBN 978 0 6482 0354 4 ISBN eBook Amazon
Audiobook: www.audible.com.au/pd/Shadows-of-Olive-Trees-Audiobook
soundcloud.com/voicesoftoday/shadows-of-olive-trees-sample

Secret symbol hidden in a stolen locket.

Desperate race through bombed streets of Budapest.

Truths that must be unveiled.

Heroes of the Secret Underground is compelling, thrilling, shocking, fast paced and a page-turner. An innovative time slip that takes the heroes from a quirky historic old hotel in the International Year of Peace 2000 to the Holocaust, Budapest in 1944.

A roller coaster of adventure that causes hearts to thump, sink, rise and finally to rejoice as memorable characters not only survive a world turned into chaos by war and inhumanity but save others.

Part autobiography, history, fantasy it is a journey like no others.

'It will be impossible to stop reading, and when you finish the book you'll find the insights and compassion stay with you always, as do those you have met within its pages. As Susanne weaves in stories from her family's secrets, she writes about the essence of humanity.'
Jackie French AM, Australian Laureate and Australian of the Year

sgervay.com/heroes-of-the-secret-underground
ISBN 978 1 4607 5833 5

As the child of refugees, I write to unlock pathways for young people to be heroes. We all need to be heroes, don't we?

Inspired by my parents and the courage of so many who endured unspeakable atrocities but never lost hope, *Heroes of the Secret Underground* challenges young people and old to become advocates of justice.

At the World Holocaust Forum Prince Charles said 'The lessons of the Holocaust are searingly relevant to this day. More than seventy-five years after the Liberation of Auschwitz-Birkenau, hatred and intolerance still lurk in the human heart, still tell new lies, adopt new disguises, and still seek new victims.'

'We must continue to empower our young people to vigorously oppose the ongoing spread of hatred and bigotry that is still so prevalent. Encouraging our readers to examine and reflect upon the past is one powerful way to do this. *Heroes of the Secret Underground* has my highest recommendation.' *Sue Warren, Reviewer and Librarian*

'It's a story of light and love and exceptional courage.' *Ursula Dubosarsky, Australian Laureate*

Thank you always to my beautiful family and extended family for your love. Thank you to HarperCollins Australia in supporting this project. To honour Ukraine.

facebook.com/sgervay instagram.com/susanne_gervay
twitter.com/sgervay linkedin.com/in/susanne-gervay-4738492

'Heart wrenching and beautiful are the two words that immediately came to mind … Gervay paints a picture of Katherine as she grows and changes allowing the reader to believe in her as a real person. Unlike other teen angst books, Katherine…chooses…to find joy in her daily life. …Katherine wins at the end – not because she suddenly becomes amazingly beautiful, but because she always was beautiful and knew that within herself. Kudos to Gervay.'
Swon Libraries

'Compelling? Moving? Inspirational? You're not even close to the power that *Butterflies* holds…Susanne Gervay has crafted this book beautifully and its gift of strength and hope will stay with the reader long after the book is put down.' *REACT Magazine*

Butterflies is a powerful coming-of-age journey of Katherine. As she meets the challenges of her accident, she searches for love, friendships and her dreams for the future.

sgervay.com/butterflies

ISBN 0 207 19850 0   ISBN 978 1 61067 043 2